Unequally Yoked

Ginna Andrew

Acknowledgement

First, I want to thank God for His grace, which has enabled and sustained me throughout the journey of writing this book.

To my husband Stephen, and my family, your unwavering encouragement and belief in me has been a constant source of strength. Thank you for always standing by my side.

A heartfelt thank you to my mum, Rose, for her love, wisdom, and continuous prayers.

To my Dominion City London Church Family, you have been a pillar of support. In particular, I extend my deepest gratitude to Pastor Ikenna Duru for his masterful sermons and his call to excellence, urging God's children to turn the dreams He has placed in our hearts into reality.

A special shout-out to my sister Danma and my colleague and friend Anne-Marie, my very first readers—your feedback and encouragement were invaluable. To Mr and Mrs Sterling, thank you for being my models.

To all who have played a role in this journey—thank you.

Dedication

To my son Ghian and my step-daughters, Seanna and Shiloh. May you always remember that you can be both holy and successful.

It is also for all God-fearing men and women who are courageously defying the rules of society and choosing to live a life honouring God. May you continue to shine as beacons of faith, strength, and purpose.

Chapter 1

Flee from sexual immorality. All other sins a person commits are outside the body, but whoever sins sexually sins against their own body.

-1 Corinthians 6:18

4:30 am Monday

Dominic Pascale Jr. rolled over in the plush embrace of the king-size bed, the crisp linen cool against his skin in the exclusive penthouse at Hotel De Capri. He glanced down at his companion; her form draped in tangled sheets and felt the familiar wave of disgust rise in his chest—disgust with himself more than her.

He knew her type. They always came to him with the same glint in their eyes, drawn by his wealth, his name, and the allure of his carefully cultivated mystique. They flirted, lingered, and hoped to ensnare him, to become the next "Mrs Pascale" and claim what they thought was his heart. He smirked bitterly. Fools. They didn't realise there was nothing left to claim. His heart had died the day Isabella had.

A trace of vanilla, her perfume from last night, filled the air and for a fleeting second, it stirred another memory. Isabella had once loved a similar perfume, its delicate floral notes lingering in her wake like a ghost of her presence. The pang in his chest was sharp and unwelcome. With a deliberate shake of his head, he pushed the thought away.

Outside, the first light of dawn broke through the thick drapes, casting a soft glow across the room. Careful not to wake the woman, whose name he couldn't remember, he rose from the bed and walked to the large windows. As he looked out, the emptiness he'd ignored all night crept back, an aching within him that nothing seemed to fill.

He poured himself a glass of whiskey from the crystal decanter on the side table, the amber liquid catching the morning light with a raw, unpolished brilliance. It carried the rugged scent of charred oak and leather, underpinned by a bold smokiness that spoke of untamed landscapes.

He took a deliberate sip, the sharp edge hitting his tongue before cascading into a deep, earthy burn that carved its way down his throat like fire meeting steel. This was his routine: wake up, reflect, and numb the pain.

The penthouse was his sanctuary, a gilded cage where he escaped the world, not the bittersweet memories. A soft groan from the bed pulled him back to reality. The woman was waking up. He took another swig of whiskey, finishing the glass and placing it down with a deliberate thud.

"It's time for you to leave," he said coldly, his voice devoid of emotion. Her eyes reflected shame and disappointment as she regarded him. She quickly gathered her things, mumbling an awkward goodbye while leaving the room.

As the door clicked shut, Dominic stared at it. He was alone again, but he preferred it that way. Attachments were dangerous, love a luxury he had to forgo. The penthouse, with all its trappings of indulgence, was a stage, and Dominic its sole performer. Here, behind closed doors, the performance continued; a man of control, of mystery, of excess. Only the lingering silence knew the truth of his loneliness.

He entered the bathroom; the steam rising as he turned on the shower. The hot water flowed over his skin, cleansing the dirt from the night, the image of the unknown woman, and the memories clinging to the outskirts of his mind.

Later, he dressed swiftly, slipping into his perfectly tailored suit, the fabric settling over his shoulders like armour. His gaze lingered on the rumpled bed momentarily before he picked up his phone and wallet from the nightstand. When he exited the penthouse, the soft click of the door shutting behind him echoed louder than it should in the silent hallway.

The air outside the suite was cool, a sharp contrast to the stifling heat of the penthouse. The night's brief passion was already slipping away, leaving behind only the hollow echo of another meaningless encounter.

Dominic, having reached the elevator, pressed the button for the ground floor; his movements were precise, almost mechanical. As the doors slid shut, he stood motionless, his posture rigid, his spine unwavering. His eyes fluttered shut, and he drew in a measured breath, releasing it slowly, attempting to still the storm of thoughts churning in his mind. The gentle hum of the descending elevator became his only solace, a fragile shield against the chaos within.

As the elevator descended, Dominic's thoughts drifted unbidden to his father. The elder Pascale had built an empire brick by brick, sealing deals with a sharp intellect and an iron will. Growing up in the vast shadow of such a figure had been both a privilege and a burden.

The empire Dominic now commanded was a monument to his father's relentless ambition. Dominic had craved his father's attention, but indifference crushed those hopes. By adulthood, he had stopped seeking approval from a man who saw him only as a tool to carry on the family name. To Pascale Senior, Dominic wasn't a son, just a means to expand the empire.

Even in death, his father's shadow loomed large. Five years ago, when Pascale Senior passed away, he left not just an empire but an unspoken mandate: *Expand. Protect. Excel.* Dominic bore the responsibility of this unspoken mandate in every decision and every boardroom.

At 31, Dominic had spent the past five years proving he was his father's equal. Yet, no amount of success could silence the question that haunted him: Was this life truly his, or just the fulfilment of his father's vision?

The elevator doors slid open, and Dominic strode through the lobby, his polished shoes clicking against the marble floor. Outside, the stylish black automobile glinted off the climbing morning sunlight waiting at the curb. He slid into the backseat, the familiar leather interior wrapping him in a cocoon of solitude, the door shutting with a solid thunk.

"Home, Mr Pascale?" the driver inquired, looking in the rearview.

"Yes, home," his tone neutral, eyes locked on the world beyond the tinted glass.

London's streets buzzed to life, commuters hurried by, cafés opened their doors, and the city thrummed with its usual energy. But Dominic felt detached, like a spectator watching life unfold around him without actually being part of it.

Inevitably, his thoughts returned to Isabella. She had been his grounding force, the sole person who had seen beyond the façade of wealth and power to the man beneath. With her, he had felt truly known. Her absence left an emptiness no fleeting encounter could complete. The women who shared his nights now were beautiful but hollow, their company a temporary escape from the ache that lingered.

Dominic leaned back, the low rumble of the engine blending into the muted sounds of the city. His Knightsbridge home loomed ahead; imposing, immaculate, and lifeless. As the iron gates clanged shut behind him, the sound reverberated through the silence, a stark reminder of the solitude that permeated his life.

His hand resting on the cold brass handle, Dominic paused before the heavy oak door. In its polished surface, he caught his faint reflection, a man impeccably dressed, every detail of his appearance curated to perfection. But as he stared, he saw the hollowness behind his sharp features, a man who had everything yet felt as though he had nothing. He took a long breath, the weight in his chest pressing harder, and turned the handle, stepping inside.

Inside, the silence engulfed him like a thick blanket. The rhythmic tick of the grandfather clock in the foyer echoed faintly, each sound dissipating into the vast, empty house. It was a solitude he had grown accustomed to over the past 18 months, a companion that offered no comfort, only a constant ache for his losses.

He proceeded to the study, pushing open the mahogany door. The recognisable scent of leather-bound books and faint wood polish greeted him, a small balm against the encroaching void. Sunlight filtered through the tall windows, casting amber streaks across the spines of books neatly lining the shelves. The room, meticulously organised, remained his refuge, a place where he could think or avoid thinking.

For a short time, the space offered him a flicker of solace. But even here, where familiarity should have clung to him, there was an aching emptiness. His father's presence persisted, an unspoken shadow, embedded in the room's very essence. The rich green of the armchairs, the heavy oak desk, and the faint scuffs on the hardwood floors spoke of a legacy both empowering and stifling, a foundation more akin to a shackle.

Dominic sank into the chair behind the desk, running his hand over its smooth surface. His gaze fell on a photograph in a silver frame, a rare remnant of his youth. His mother's radiant smile dominated the image, standing in sharp contrast to his father's stern, detached expression. He picked it up, his fingers brushing the frame's edge as memories surfaced unbidden. The photograph captured one of the rare occasions his father had attended an event for him. Even then, the approval had been fleeting, transactional, leaving a boy longing for more.

A steaming cup of coffee sat on the desk, its rich aroma curling through the air. Placed with precision, it was a quiet testament to

James, his ever-attentive live-in butler. Having served the Pascale family for decades, James anticipated Dominic's needs with near-instinctive precision. The coffee was dark, bold, and bitter—much like Dominic's mood.

As he lifted the cup, Dominic felt the warmth spread to his hands. The bitterness spread across his tongue, momentarily grounding him in the present. Yet the clarity was short-lived, replaced by the ever-present haze of fatigue and disconnection.

He opened his laptop, the light from the screen casting a cold light across the dark wood. Emails filled the display, their subject lines a deluge of obligations and demands. He scrolled aimlessly; the words blurring into static, the weight of decisions looming like shadows on the periphery of his thoughts. His focus wavered, splintered by the monotony of a life that seemed both relentless and empty.

The sharp buzz of his phone shattered the quiet, a jarring intrusion that cut through the study's stillness. He peered at the screen, another reminder of the ceaseless obligations pressing in on all sides. He set the phone down unanswered, sighing and stroking his brow to relieve the mounting tension. His fingers lingered at his temple, pressing against the dull ache that had become as familiar as the silence in the room.

His gaze drifted to the walls, where neatly framed certificates and photographs hung in perfect symmetry. Diplomas from the world's top universities, awards for business excellence, and snapshots from charity galas filled the space. They painted a picture of relentless success, of a man respected and admired. Yet, to Dominic, they felt more like a carefully curated illusion—one that didn't truly reflect the man behind the image.

Finally, his eyelids fluttered shut and let his head rest against the high back of the leather chair. His loneliness pressed down on him, unyielding. The study, with its rare first editions and antique desk lamp, felt less like a sanctuary and more like a vault, a place where his achievements amplified the silence and his memories echoed too loudly.

Here, stripped of the masks he wore in boardrooms and social events, Dominic Pascale Jr. was not the celebrated CEO or the magnetic public figure. He was just a man, haunted by love and moments he could never reclaim. The memories lingered like cigar smoke in a dimly lit room, curling and dissipating into the air, leaving behind a sense of something once potent, now fading and elusive.

"What is it all for?" The question floated in the air, unanswered, as the faint tick of the clock counted the seconds of another empty day.

Chapter 2

In the morning, Lord, you hear my voice; in the morning, I lay my requests before you and wait expectantly.

-Psalms 5:3

4:30 am Monday

Danielle Thompson reached over and turned off her alarm. She rested, offering silent thanks for the new day's gift. Within minutes, she rolled out of bed, grabbed her towel, and headed for the shower. The cool water invigorated her, washing away the last traces of sleep in readiness for her church's 5:00 a.m. online prayer meeting.

Her faith was her anchor, steadying her through life's challenges. Though staying consistent wasn't always easy, her early morning prayers had become an irreplaceable part of her routine. Danielle knew the struggle of walking a different path, especially in a world that often clashed with her Christian beliefs. Yet, she also knew that with the Holy Spirit's guidance, it was not only possible, but necessary.

No one was perfect, nor was she, but Danielle approached life with a heart intent on obedience, striving to love, forgive, and treat others as she wished to be treated. Her walk with God wasn't just about rituals or rules; it was about cultivating a relationship that transformed her from within.

After her shower, she wrapped herself in a plush robe and smoothed out her sheets and pillows, a daily routine, one her mother had instilled in her as a child: *start your day with order and discipline, and the rest will follow.*

With her room tidied, she set up her laptop on the desk and logged onto the prayer call. Familiar faces filled her screen, and as the prayer session began, Danielle joined in, her voice blending with theirs in a soothing rhythm of devotion.

These moments refreshed her spirit, lifting her burdens and reminding her of the fortitude she drew from her community and her Creator. When the session ended, she lingered in the calm, a quiet confidence settling over her. It was this peace that prepared her to confront whatever the day ahead might bring.

Afterward, Danielle made herself a simple breakfast of scrambled eggs with spinach, a slice of whole-grain toast and a chamomile tea infusion. She cherished these reflective moments before the demands of the day took over. Overlooking the window from her desk, she opened her journal and wrote.

Today, her thoughts flowed effortlessly. She expressed gratitude for her new role at Pascale & Pascale, her health, her family and the supportive friends who always stood by her. Focusing on these blessings helped her approach to life with clarity and intention, even amidst its challenges.

At 27, Danielle had accomplished much through dedication and perseverance. Earning a position as a Senior Financial Analyst at one of London's top financial firms was a major milestone—a testament to her hard work. It was more than just a career move; it was an opportunity to prove her expertise in a fiercely competitive industry.

She thought of the CEO of Pascale & Pascale, Dominic Pascale. His name carried immense recognition in the financial, but mostly, the tabloids fixated on his personal life, painting a picture of a playboy billionaire who navigated life with a devil-may-care attitude and an endless string of glamorous women.

Danielle reminded herself that her role focused firmly on data and reports, and she was unlikely to interact with someone as high-ranking as the CEO. Still, the thought of him had persisted in her subconscious ever since she accepted the job.

Maybe it was the notoriety surrounding his name or the sheer magnetism of the stories about him. She took a steadying breath. He's just a man, she thought firmly. Confidently, she closed her journal, ready to embrace a new chapter in her life.

Chapter 3

I praise you, for I am fearfully and wonderfully made. Wonderful are your works; my soul knows it very well.

-Psalms 139:14

Danielle had taken her time this morning to ensure that she looked her best to make a good impression. She wore a white, tailored Pinko two-piece suit. Its wide-leg trousers and peplum-style jacket created a sleek yet feminine silhouette that perfectly blended corporate formality and a hint of relaxed elegance. The suit's modest cut reflected her Christian values, with the jacket gently cinching her waist and skimming over her hips, ensuring she felt confident yet comfortable.

She styled her hair in a half-up, half-down sweep, softly framing her face, and small silver studs adorned her earlobes, adding just the right amount of subtle elegance. A swipe of her favourite brown-hued lipstick accentuated her natural features, paired with a light coat of mascara to make her eyes pop, her sleeked eyebrows completing the polished look.

She slipped on her Christian Louboutin, her most cherished gift from her exuberant best friend, Tenille, affectionately known as "Ten." As she caught her reflection in the mirror, a smile touched her lips. She looked and felt good, the kind of good that came from a sense of purpose and inner peace.

Quickly grabbing her black Birkin tote bag, she secured the door and got into the waiting Uber, whispering a prayer. "God, please protect me on my journey today and grant me favour with my new colleagues. Help me represent you in all my endeavours." Her words, though brief, were heartfelt, as she trusted in God's guidance and presence.

The cab rolled smoothly through the streets, the city alive with activity, people hurrying to work, the sounds of traffic and the excitement of a new dawn unfolding. It was a familiar rhythm, one that left her feeling connected to something bigger.

She inhaled deeply, mentally preparing herself for her first day at work. With every passing moment, she felt more grounded, knowing that no matter what challenges the day would bring, she was prepared to confront it.

Danielle arrived at the towering headquarters and a familiar sense of awe washed over her, just as it had during her interview. The building loomed like a monument to success, its sleek glass facade mirroring the ceaseless energy of the financial district.

Stepping inside, she saw a hive of activity; employees moved with purpose, their expressions sharp with determination. The steady hum of conversation mixed with the rhythmic click of heels on polished floors, a sound that pulsed in sync with the company's relentless drive.

After clearing security and receiving her key card, Danielle stepped into the lift and ascended to the 14th floor, home to the Finance Team. The foyer exuded modern sophistication—polished glass walls gleamed under sleek lighting, minimalist furniture was arranged with precision, and the atmosphere carried a quiet, focused energy.

As she walked through the foyer, Danielle was keenly sensitive to the stares trailing her. It was nothing new; she had long grown accustomed to the scrutiny. Being a woman of colour in a male-dominated field was no novelty to her, but it came with its own set of challenges. Her dreadlocks, meticulously styled, were more than a hairstyle; they were a proud declaration of her heritage and identity. She knew they often sparked curiosity and judgment, but she carried them with pride, refusing to let the weight of others' perceptions settle on her shoulders.

Standing out in a crowd was something she had learned to accept, whether it was for her cultural background or her striking beauty. Danielle understood her true value had nothing to do with appearances. Her faith, sharp intellect and unwavering integrity rooted her self-worth, and she brought this to every room she entered.

Those who underestimated her would soon realise their mistake; she had no intention of being defined by anyone's expectations but her own. She was wonderfully and beautifully created by God, both a queen and a priest, set apart, called to lead and make a difference wherever life placed her.

Today, as Danielle stepped into the world of Pascale & Pascale, she was determined to show exactly who she was. She approached this new chapter with cautious optimism, hoping this workplace would be different. After all, the firm's founder and CEO were from an ethnic minority, which had led her to believe that diversity and inclusion weren't just corporate buzzwords here, but real values woven into the company's culture.

Despite corporate efforts to align with the rhetoric of diversity, reality often told a different story. Danielle understood that true representation went beyond simply hiring people from different backgrounds. A deeper cultural shift was needed, one where the organisation gave women and minorities genuine opportunities to advance, valued their voices, and actively sought their perspectives. There was still a long way to go.

Danielle wasn't one to back down. If this workplace wasn't what she had hoped, she resolved to leave her mark in ways that mattered, to pave a path for herself and for others who would follow.

As the lift doors slid open, she involuntarily recalled her last visit. The 15th floor, just above, housed the litigation department. The hushed corridors of the litigation department held a heavier, more austere energy, a place where people wielded words as weapons. Precision mattered, and tension seemed to hum in the air.

Beyond that, the 16th floor was a different realm altogether: the CEO's office, the epicentre of power. There, people sealed high-stakes deals, crafted strategies, and making far-reaching impact. The idea sent a ripple of awe through her.

Each floor reflected its function, a hierarchy of purpose and authority. As the lift ascended, Danielle sensed the significance of it all—the buzz of finance, the sharp edge of litigation, and the commanding authority of the top. With a soft ding, the lift stopped, and she walked into the world that would soon be her own.

When Danielle finally stepped into her office, she was completely mesmerised. The space was a perfect fusion of modern luxury and refined elegance. A sleek coffee machine rested on a quartz counter, its polished surface gleaming under the soft lighting, promising warmth and comfort during long workdays.

A plush sofa beckoned, offering a retreat for quiet reflection or a brief escape from the daily grind. But it was the desk that commanded attention, an imposing masterpiece of polished wood, exuding both authority and sophistication.

She pulled the blinds open with a soft swoosh, revealing a sweeping vista of the river winding through the city. The tranquil River Thames beneath the morning sun created a perfect contrast to the energetic pulse of the city. It was both grounding and awe-inspiring.

She couldn't resist a little celebratory twirl. The office was everything she'd imagined and more. Overcome with excitement, she pulled out her phone and took a quick video of the space, capturing every angle; the polished floors, the sleek furniture, and the breathtaking view, sending it to her mum Rose and her friends Ten and Naomi.

Danielle bowed her head in quiet reverence, the stillness of the room amplifying the sincerity of her prayer. Gratitude surged within her—gratitude for the opportunity, for the new chapter unfolding, and for the strength that sustained her this far. She thanked God for His unwavering guidance and protection, asking Him to bless this space and make it a sanctuary where His presence could dwell.

She knew the importance of keeping her faith at the centre of everything she did, especially in the workplace. Having faced difficult people and situations before, Danielle recognised that spiritual battles often appeared as negativity and hostility. By dedicating this space to God through prayer, she wasn't just claiming it for herself—she was inviting His protection, wisdom, and peace into every interaction, decision, and challenge that lay ahead.

Moments later, a knock sounded at the door. "Enter," she announced, her voice steady but tinged with curiosity. The door swung open, and a well-dressed woman with a warm smile entered. She was holding a bouquet and a small card.

"Hello, Danielle! I'm Emily, the office coordinator. Welcome to Pascale & Pascale." She handed over a beautifully wrapped bouquet with a warm smile. "These are from the team."

Danielle stood, her smile wide. "Thank you so much, Emily. This is very kind."

Emily handed her the flowers and card, then glanced around the office with appreciation. "I hope your first day goes well. Should you require anything, reach out."

"I appreciate that," Danielle said, as she took the flowers and set them on the desk. Emily gave her a last nod and left, leaving Danielle alone once more.

She opened the small card and smiled as she read the handwritten message from her new colleagues. It was warm and welcoming, a simple but meaningful gesture putting her at ease.

"Welcome to the team, Danielle! We're so excited to have you here. Looking forward to working with you. - The Financial Team."

She admired the flowers for a moment, inhaling their sweet fragrance before gently placing the card beside them. The small, thoughtful gesture made the office feel homier, something she truly appreciated.

Her manager, Mr Anderson, soon arrived and welcome her officially and summarising her initial responsibilities.

"Danielle, we're thrilled to have you on board," Mr Anderson said warmly. "I know you'll be an invaluable addition to our team. Let's start with a brief orientation, and then I'll introduce you to the remaining team."

The orientation went smoothly, and Danielle rapidly found herself immersed in the rhythm of her new role. Her colleagues were professional and friendly, though she could sense their curiosity. She knew it would take time to build relationships and earn their respect, but she was confident in her abilities.

As the day unfolded, Danielle settled into her role, tackling her tasks with quiet confidence. Entrusted with several reports to review and analyse, she immersed herself in the work, her focus sharp and unwavering. Her keen attention to detail and critical thinking quickly became clear, and it wasn't long before her colleagues took notice.

Just before lunch, Mr Anderson stopped by her office again, offering her a warm smile. "How's everything going so far?" he asked, leaning against the doorframe.

"Everything's going great, Mr Anderson," Danielle said with a warm smile. "The team has been incredibly welcoming, and I'm excited to dive into the upcoming projects."

"I'm glad to hear that," he said. "You're going to be working on some high-level projects imminently. I believe you'll fit right in. We have a big client meeting coming up and we could use your expertise."

Danielle's lunch break offered a moment of quiet introspection as she sat in the bustling cafeteria. In her journal, she jotted down a few thoughts about her first day while sipping her water. Grateful, yet aware, she wrote. Today feels like a fresh start. I can do this. The work is challenging, but I've been prepared for this. God has placed me here for a reason.

After lunch, Danielle returned to her office, ready to immerse herself in the financial reports assigned to her. The work demanded focus, and she quickly lost herself in the numbers, her mind sharp and analytical. A surge of excitement ran through her. This was exactly the challenge she thrived on.

Later that afternoon, Danielle's phone buzzed on her desk. "Hi, Danielle. Emily here. You have a meeting scheduled for 4:00pm in the 16th-floor conference room. It's with the CEO and a few other senior executives. I can show you the way if you'd like."

"Thank you, Emily. I appreciate it. Could you come for me ten minutes before the meeting, to show me the way, please?"

"Of course," Emily responded.

Danielle stepped into the shower room and touched up her makeup, carefully reapplying her lipstick and smoothing her foundation. No matter the emotions swirling inside her, she needed to look poised and professional.

So much for avoiding Dominic Pascale, she thought wryly. The thought of seeing him stirred a mix of excitement, trepidation, and the weight of expectation, all colliding at once. She took a steadying breath, willing herself to stay composed. "Pull yourself together, Danielle," she murmured to her reflection.

But the reality was undeniable. She was about to meet a high-profile CEO—a man whose reputation and influence loomed over the company. And despite her confidence, the pressure to make a powerful impression pressed down on her.

She took a few more deep breaths and closed her eyes and whispered a brief prayer, seeking divine guidance and strength. "Father, your will be done. Give me courage, insightful guidance, and understanding and your favour upon me as I attend this meeting. Amen."

Shortly after, Emily knocked on her door.

"Hi Danielle, are you ready?"

"Yes," she replied, "lead the way."

Emily led Danielle out of her office and toward the elevators. As they ascended to the 16th floor, they chatted briefly about the upcoming meeting. Emily, ever helpful, shared a few insights on navigating the senior executive environment, offering subtle yet valuable tips. Danielle listened intently, mentally preparing herself for what lay ahead.

As the elevator doors slid open at the sixteenth level, Danielle felt her pulse quicken. The floor was sleek and modern, with polished floors and windows reaching the ceiling that gave a panoramic view of the city. Emily led the way through a corridor lined with closed doors, stopping in front of one that had a sign reading, "Executive Boardroom."

"Here we are," Emily said. "Good luck, Danielle!"

Chapter 4

The wicked flee though no one pursues, but the righteous are as bold as a lion.

-Proverbs 28:1

Dominic Pascale stood in the sleek, modern conference room, his gaze drifting over the panoramic cityscape beyond the floor-to-ceiling windows. The view was impressive, but his mind was elsewhere. He glanced at the meticulously organised schedule his assistant had prepared, skimming through the day's agenda.

His final meeting stood out—a session with the senior executives and an introduction to the new Senior Financial Analyst. It was a role he considered crucial, one that required sharp insight and precision. He hoped they had chosen well.

He had always made it a point to meet employees in senior roles, and this was no exception. The role included analysing financial data, forecasting trends, assisting with budgeting, and advising management. Dominic wanted to make his assessment of the young woman filling this role.

From what he had gathered, the hiring manager had spoken highly of her sharp attention to detail and the impressive experience she brought from Chase & Bear. Her CV was undeniably strong, a testament to her expertise and ambition. Yet, one detail stood out to Dominic, her departure from such a prestigious bank. Especially when they had fought to keep her. He wondered what prompted her to leave.

His focus would be to test her financial acumen and see if her qualifications and experience matched the high expectations of the role. He checked his watch and saw that it was 3:45 pm. The financial controller, along with the executive senior team, would begin arriving shortly. It would be interesting to observe whether the new analyst maintains the crucial punctuality expected.

After his meeting, Dominic had plans to have dinner at 7:00 pm with his childhood friend Vivienne Fox. He frowned as he thought about their upcoming rendezvous. Vivienne was undeniably attractive, but Dominic found himself increasingly frustrated by the lack of depth in their relationship.

He knew she harboured some affection for him, which only complicated matters. Dominic could not see her as a suitable life partner despite her charm. The prospect of a marriage that resembled a business transaction than a genuine union was not something he was prepared to entertain.

He had long accepted the idea that there would be no one else after Isabella. Her memory remained a bittersweet reminder of the love and depth he had once known, a love that felt irreplaceable. The thought of finding anything even remotely comparable seemed more distant with each passing year, an illusion he no longer dared to chase.

Dominic sighed and refocused on the day's schedule. His focus needed to remain sharp, as the financial health of the company and his team's performance were paramount. He would have to address his personal complexities after his professional responsibilities.

Shortly after, the executives filed into the room, taking their seats around the long, polished wooden table. Quiet murmurs filled the space, but no one attempted to engage Dominic in conversation, they knew better.

The Chief Financial Officer (CFO) would lead the meeting, steering discussions on the company's financial viability for the quarter. Among the key agenda points was the introduction of the new Senior Financial Analyst, a role critical to the firm's continued success.

Dominic stood with his back towards the rest of the room, gazing out at the scenic view. He appeared deep in thought, his reflection mirrored in the glass. Suddenly, the glass doors of the conference room swung open. Danielle strode in confidently, her entrance commanding attention, and all eyes swivelled towards her.

Upon Danielle's arrival, she felt the room's attention shift toward her and she instinctively straightened her posture. An undeniable tension hung in the air, one that came with walking into a room full of high-level executives, but the real challenge was the seat next to the head of the table.

It was apparent that she had to sit beside Dominic Pascale, the very man who had been the subject of countless tabloid headlines. She could feel her stomach tighten as she approached the seat. Taking a breath, she sat impeccably in the empty chair and smiled at the room.

She suppressed a brief nervous flutter, determined to remain composed. She knew Dominic was there, despite him not turning. His reputation as a charismatic yet elusive CEO loomed large.

Danielle made a conscious effort not to glance his way as she settled into her seat. Her attention was instead on the materials before her, organising her notes and keeping her attention outward. She was here to prove herself, not to get entangled in anything that could distract from her work.

Meanwhile, Dominic's eyes widened as Danielle entered the room, her presence commanding his full attention. In an instant, the quiet authority she exuded caught him off guard. There was something magnetic about her poised stride, the effortless grace in her movements, the calm confidence she carried. It wasn't just striking, it was impossible to ignore.

As she approached the empty seat next to his, Dominic had an unexpected visceral reaction. When Danielle sat and offered the room a genuine, unguarded smile, it pierced through the carefully constructed shell around his soul. There was no artifice in her expression, just authenticity.

It cracked the shell, but rather than soften, he recoiled. The sudden wave of vulnerability angered him, shaking the foundation of his control. He tightened his jaw, his reaction raw and untempered, though he couldn't look away.

It was 4:00 pm sharp, and everyone knew Dominic's reputation for punctuality. Without a word, he turned and walked to the top of the table, his movements precise, his presence commanding. His rigid posture and sharp gestures didn't contain the tension he carried, it hung heavy and almost tangible in the air, captivating everyone in the room.

When he sat down, his eyes briefly flicked to Danielle, their gazes locked momentarily, and a spark of something unspoken passed between them. It was enough to unsettle him, though he quickly masked it. Danielle's calm, unwavering demeanour was unexpected, and it threw him off balance.

Dominic was proud of his skill in reading people, to gauge their intentions and emotions, before they uttered a word. Yet Danielle was a mystery. He expected the usual signs; anxious smiles, timid attempts at small talk, but there was none of that. There was no trace of hesitation in her, no nervous energy, no furtive glances his way. Instead, she exuded a steady, unshakable presence, which only deepened his intrigue.

Danielle met Dominic's eyes, and his gaze unsettled her. It lingered like a touch, making her shift slightly, struggling to appear composed while tension coiled inside her. Dominic Pascale was more imposing than she had expected; his presence was sharp, unyielding, and impossible to ignore. Determined to focus, Danielle would let her work speak for itself. Yet, the tension between them was impossible to ignore.

"Good afternoon," he began, his voice cutting through the air, firm, commanding, and curt. "Let's get started. We have important matters to discuss today."

The room snapped to attention. Danielle steadied herself, ready to prove her place at the table, even as her pulse quickened under the pressure of his presence. The CFO, Barbara Johnson, introduced Danielle with a curt nod, signalling it was her turn to speak. Danielle stood, her movements fluid and assured, scanning the room before beginning her introduction.

"Good afternoon, I'm Danielle Thompson. I look forward to collaborating with all of you and contributing to our strategic objectives." Her voice was steady, carrying an effortless self-assurance that commanded attention. There was no arrogance, just a quiet confidence that exuded competence and control, leaving no doubt that she belonged in the room.

Dominic, reclining in his chair, watched her closely. Determined to test the calm exterior she presented so effortlessly, he interjected. "So, Ms Thompson," he remarked, his tone cutting and deliberate, "you're looking forward to playing a part in our strategic plans. What exactly are those?" he asked, the challenge clear.

Danielle faltered for a split second, surprised by the abruptness of the question, but quickly recovered. She raised her head, meeting Dominic's piercing gaze head-on, cool and composed.

"Certainly, Mr Pascale," Danielle responded smoothly. "Our strategic goals focus on strengthening financial performance through in-depth analysis and forecasting, identifying promising investment opportunities, and maintaining a strong risk management framework. My role is to deliver accurate, timely financial insights that support informed decision-making, ultimately driving sustainable growth and profitability." Her words were precise, her delivery flawless. She had parried his challenge with grace and control, allowing no opportunity for reproach.

Dominic felt a flicker of both frustration and reluctant admiration. Her response had been a masterclass in professionalism, measured, confident, and unwavering. Yet, for him, it felt personal. She had answered his challenge, refusing to waver, and unsettled him in a way he hadn't experienced in years. It was a rare moment of vulnerability, one he hadn't allowed himself to feel since Isabella.

"Well, Ms Thompson, I'm eager to see how you contribute to those goals," he retorted dismissively. "Let's see if your actions match your words."

"Thank you, Mr Pascale. I'm confident they will." Danielle replied politely.

As Barbara presented the financial data and forecasts, Dominic leaned back in his chair, listening intently. His gaze occasionally flickered to Danielle, noting the precision in her movements, the way she meticulously jotted down notes, her subtle nods of agreement with the CFO's points. Her focus was razor sharp, each detail absorbed with unwavering attentiveness. It was clear she was fully engaged.

As the meeting unfolded, Dominic found his intrigue deepening. Danielle's questions were incisive, her grasp of the company's financial intricacies precise and thought-provoking. Despite the initial spark of annoyance he had felt, he couldn't deny her acumen, or the understated power she brought to the table. It was rare for anyone to impress him so quickly. However, she was holding her ground and commanding respect without fanfare.

Meanwhile, Barbara maintained her polished composure, but beneath the surface, frustration simmered. Dominic's tone toward Danielle had been sharper than necessary—something she had picked up on the moment the meeting began.

Having observed him closely for three years, Barbara knew Dominic Pascale to be professional, even-tempered, and rarely governed by emotion. But with Danielle, something was different. There was an undercurrent of tension, a subtle but undeniable charge in the way he engaged with her. It wasn't just scrutiny; it was deeper, something uncharacteristic, and that unsettled Barbara.

Barbara had long considered herself the epitome of poise and professionalism. Her tailored suits, perfectly styled hair, and unshakable confidence had always commanded attention, especially from men in power. She had been careful to show her interest in Dominic. Never overt, but just enough to plant the idea. Yet, despite her efforts, he barely spared her a glance.

And now here was Danielle. With her natural locs, effortless elegance, and quiet confidence, she had stirred something in Dominic that Barbara never could. It was maddening. No matter how polished or capable Barbara was, Danielle had walked in and disrupted the unshakable Dominic Pascale, and that was something Barbara couldn't ignore.

It wasn't merely Dominic's reaction that gnawed at Barbara. Danielle's contributions to the discussion were undeniable. She was intelligent, articulate, and brimming with fresh ideas that seemed to resonate in the room. Worse, Dominic noticed. His occasional nods of approval, a spark of intrigue in his eyes, all pointed to the fact that Danielle was making an impact and not just on the company.

Unbeknownst to Danielle, she had just made her first enemy. Barbara's gaze narrowed as she watched the new analyst with growing resentment. She noted every question Danielle answered with ease, every moment she captured the room's attention. A storm of jealousy and determination brewing within her.

Barbara resolved to keep a close watch on Danielle. She wouldn't allow this newcomer to upend the carefully constructed world she had worked so relentlessly to build. If Danielle wanted a place at Pascale & Pascale, she would have to earn it and Barbara would make sure it wouldn't come easy.

Dominic found his thoughts straying, unable to fully immerse himself in the meeting. Danielle's poised demeanour, sharp responses, and the curious pull she seemed to have on him kept looping in his mind. He had built a career and a reputation for staying detached and unemotional, reading people with precision and maintaining control.

But she unsettled that balance with nothing more than her presence and composure.

As the discussion drew to a close, Dominic quietly resolved to keep a close eye on her. Danielle was an unknown variable he hadn't expected, a wild card in his world of calculated risks and carefully crafted strategies. And Dominic didn't like surprises. If she was going to remain in his orbit, he needed to understand her—both professionally and personally.

When the meeting concluded, Danielle, unaware of the stir she had caused, felt a quiet sense of achievement. The tension and challenges hadn't rattled her, and she had shown herself capable and confident. While Dominic's probing question had been unexpected, her response had been well-received. She had done her part, and that was enough for her.

When she departed the conference room, she gave herself a figurative gentle tap on her shoulders. She was content, ready to return to her desk to tie up a few loose ends before heading home. Danielle offered a silent prayer of gratitude for the day's triumphs and challenges as she walked through the office corridors.

This was just the start, she reminded herself. She had claimed her space, met the first of many hurdles, and planted the seeds for her success. Growth and opportunity lay ahead, and she was committed to making her mark, one step at a time.

Chapter 5

Do not enter the path of the wicked, and do not walk in the way of the evil.
Avoid it; do not go on it; turn away from it and pass on.

-Proverbs 4:14-15

Danielle stepped into her four-bedroom home in the affluent neighbourhood of Wanstead, London. The familiar scent of fresh flowers from her garden blended with the delicate aroma of essential oils, creating a soothing welcome. She kicked off her heels by the entryway, exhaling a deep sigh of relief. Home was her sanctuary and stepping inside felt like shedding the pressures of the outside world.

The house was her haven, a space she had carefully crafted over the years. When she bought the property, Wanstead was still relatively undiscovered, but now it was a sought-after neighbourhood, with house prices soaring.

She loved the home's natural décor, modern touches like the surround sound system, and its spacious layout. One bedroom served as her office and prayer room, a sacred space where she centred herself. She had converted another bedroom into a library to house her extensive book collection.

Danielle went to her en-suite bedroom, a space that blended elegance with comfort. The enormous bed, adorned with a cloud-like duvet and meticulously arranged throw pillows, dominated the room. Cream and gold tones gave it a calming ambiance, complemented by her favourite art pieces on the walls. A plush, luxurious rug cushioned her steps, while the dimmed lighting bathed the space in a warm, inviting glow.

She walked into her bathroom, her personal retreat. It was sleek and indulgent, designed for relaxation. The walk-in shower with its rainfall showerhead was her favourite feature. Shelves lined with fragrant bath products; jasmine, vanilla, and sandalwood added a touch of luxury. As the warm water cascaded over her, the tension of the day dissolved. The rhythmic flow provided solace, like a balm, soothing her mind and body.

Refreshed, Danielle stepped into her walk-in closet, a perfect blend of organisation and elegance. Her wardrobe was meticulously arranged by colour and occasion. Rows of designer shoes, heels, sneakers, and boots, stood in neat formation, an army of options ready for any event. Shelves showcased her collection of handbags, each carrying a memory, a milestone in time.

A light aroma of lavender from a nearby diffuser filled the air, adding to the serene ambiance of her personal retreat. In the closet's corner stood a full-length mirror, reflecting the harmonious elegance of the room. Danielle often paused there to admire an outfit or silently acknowledge her journey and growth.

As she dried off and slipped into something comfortable, Danielle's mind replayed the day's events. Meeting Dominic Pascale had left a lasting impression—his piercing gaze, effortless authority, and the quiet intensity that surrounded him. He was undeniably striking, but it was his commanding presence that truly unsettled her.

"Intimidating is an understatement," she muttered, reaching for her favourite lavender-scented lotion, its calming aroma easing her nerves. Despite his obvious irritation during their exchange, she had held her ground. A small smile tugged at her lips. She was proud of herself for standing firm under his unrelenting scrutiny.

Danielle headed to the kitchen to prepare a light dinner. Danielle's kitchen was the heart of her home, bright and meticulously organised. The soft light from pendant lights illuminated the space as she moved gracefully, slicing zucchini and bell peppers with practised ease. Tonight, she was making her favourite stir-fry, a simple yet flavourful dish that always left her feeling satisfied and recharged.

As she sautéed the vegetables in sesame oil, the fragrant aroma filled the room, blending with the gentle strains of gospel music playing in the background. Cooking had always been therapy for her, a way to channel her thoughts and reconnect after a long day. It allowed her to reflect without distractions, her hands busy while her mind found clarity.

Suddenly, her phone rang.

"Did you see the ravishing Mr Pascale?" Ten's voice crackled with excitement.

Danielle chuckled, shaking her head. "Hi, Ten. I'm very well, thank you! My first day was wonderful. Thanks for asking. Yes, I met Mr Pascale. Girl, I'm in so much trouble. Pray for me!'"

"Haha, what happened? Spill!" Ten replied eagerly.

Danielle paused, as if searching for the right words. "He's far more striking than any photograph could capture, a face chiselled with precision, every angle sculpted by an artist. His impeccably groomed beard and moustache frame full lips that speak of quiet authority."

"His brown skin radiates a warmth, a richness that's magnetic. But it's his eyes. They're soulful, like they hold untold stories and secrets that could draw you in without mercy. And his presence, it's raw and commanding. He doesn't just walk into a room; he owns it. Everyone else feels smaller in comparison."

A stunned silence followed. Danielle blinked, surprised at her own poetic outburst, while Ten remained speechless at the other side. "Dani, you weren't kidding when you said you're in trouble. Girlfriend, you are *definitely* on my prayer list tonight."

"Girl, get me on that list on the double! At the meeting, a moment of intense eye contact occurred between us. Outwardly I was calm, but inside, I was squirming. Though, on reflection, I believe he felt annoyed by me."

"Annoyed, why?"

"I don't know. It was strange. When I walked into the meeting, I could feel his gaze, like he was evaluating me. And when I sat down next to him, the air felt charged, like there was this tension, almost electric. Then, when our eyes met, he seemed angry or frustrated. I can't explain it."

"Maybe he wasn't angry at you. Perhaps that's just how he sizes people up. People in his position are probably always analysing."

"Yeah, maybe. But it was unsettling. I've met powerful people before, but he's different. Intense."

"He likes you! He wants to marry you!" Ten sang teasingly.

"Don't be ridiculous," Danielle laughed. "I can't be unequally yoked, but I see why women, Christian or not, would compete to be his next conquest." "He's captivating! But I'm here to perform my duties, not be another name in his little black book. Besides, I probably imagined it. I doubt he even noticed me beyond being part of the team."

"Dani, please. You're drop-dead gorgeous, and you have an aura about you. Trust me, he noticed."

"Even if he did, it doesn't matter. I've worked too hard to build my reputation. I'm not interested in office drama or being reduced to a statistic."

"Well said," Ten agreed. "But stay prayed up. Sometimes hearts get caught off guard."

"Will do, Ten. Thanks." With a smile, she said goodnight and hung up.

After dinner, Danielle brewed a cup of chamomile tea, its soothing aroma wrapping around her as she made her way to the library. The room was her sanctuary—floor-to-ceiling shelves lined with books on finance, personal development, fiction, and Christian literature. A warm glow from the reading lamp cast a gentle light over the cosy nook by the window, where a plush armchair and a soft throw blanket invited her to unwind.

As she settled in with her tea, she opened *Being a Key Person of Interest,* a book that had struck a chord with her from the first page. Its message about building influence while staying true to one's values resonated deeply, especially now as she navigated her new role. The words inspired her, grounding her in the importance of purpose and perspective. After finishing a couple of enlightening chapters, she closed the book and placed it on the small side table.

As was her routine, she walked across the hall to her prayer room, a serene space designed for reflection and connection with God. The room was minimal yet sacred, with soft lighting, a plush prayer mat, and a small altar adorned with a Bible and a few cherished items. As she knelt, the worries of the day faded, replaced by the quiet strength of her faith.

"Lord, thank you for this day," she prayed, her voice soft but resolute. "For the opportunities you've placed before me and the strength you've given me to embrace them. Guide me with wisdom and courage as I continue this journey. May I reflect your light in all I do and stand firm against every challenge. Amen."

With gratitude and peace filling her heart, Danielle lingered for a moment after rising from her knees. She then made her way to her bedroom, slipping beneath the inviting covers, the day's events flickering briefly in her mind. Dominic Pascale might be a force of nature, but a lioness doesn't shrink before a roar. Her drive to excel wasn't about proving herself to him or anyone else, it was a testament to her faith, integrity, and purpose.

A last word of prayer and then sleep embraced her gently, preparing her for whatever the next day would bring.

Chapter 6

And behold, a woman comes to meet him, dressed as a harlot and cunning of heart.

-Proverbs 7:10

After the meeting ended, Dominic stayed at the headquarters, tackling the mountain of work that never seemed to diminish. He was not looking forward to his rendevouz with Vivienne. Their mothers had always dreamed they'd end up together, a shared hope that Dominic had never entertained. His heart had belonged to Isabella, and 18 months after her passing, he remained a man deeply marked by that loss.

Isabella's memory was as vivid as ever. Reserved and graceful, she had insisted their engagement remain private, a reflection of her quiet nature. As the daughter of the renowned singer Isabel Biancolli, she craved a life free of the public's relentless gaze. Dominic had admired her for it and loved her all the more. Losing her had shattered him in ways he didn't think he could articulate, leaving behind an ache that time failed to dull.

Vivienne was the opposite. A vibrant, persistent force who refused to fade into the background. Their weekly meetings, he suspected, served more than just the purpose of friendly companionship. She chose high-profile venues for their outings to ensure that people saw them together, carefully crafting a public narrative, perhaps for Dominic's benefit as well.

He sighed, looking at the clock. It was nearly time to leave. While he appreciated Vivienne's loyalty and efforts, their dinners felt more like an obligation than a pleasure. As he gathered his belongings, an unexpected image of Danielle intruded, making him pause before leaving the office.

Her confident stride, her genuine smile from earlier replayed in his mind. Dominic found it infuriating. He had spent years perfecting the art of detachment, yet this new hire had broken through in a way he couldn't ignore. Not even Isabella had affected him so immediately. He shook his head, clearing his thoughts, then made his way to the car, willing himself to concentrate on the evening ahead.

The private room at Le Fleur was every bit as luxurious as expected, its muted gold and cream tones exuding quiet elegance. Vivienne sat poised as ever, her emerald-green wrap dress hugging her frame just right. She checked her watch, irritation flickering momentarily before vanishing behind a practised smile. In public, she couldn't allow herself to frown.

She sipped her glass of sparkling water, her crimson-painted lips leaving a faint mark on the rim. Despite her outward composure, a tightness constricted her chest. Dominic's distant demeanour was becoming harder to ignore. The man who once shared his thoughts so freely with her now seemed locked away behind walls she couldn't penetrate.

Vivienne wasn't a woman to cling to fantasies; she was far too practical for that. Yet, the memories of their once-easy camaraderie lingered, making her believe there was still hope. Before Isabella, she and Dominic had shared something real, she assured herself. They had understood one another's ambitions, or so she told herself.

But Isabella had changed everything. Dominic's late fiancée was everything Vivienne wasn't. Warm, unguarded, and deeply emotional. Though Vivienne never let it show, she had resented her. Yet, over time, she resigned herself to the background, waiting patiently for her moment.

After Isabella died, Vivienne had believed Dominic would finally turn to her, drawn to the stability she could offer. But that moment had not yet arrived.

Instead, he seemed further away than ever, his grief transforming into a quiet detachment. Vivienne told herself to be calm, that he would see her as his logical choice in time. Love wasn't what being Mrs Pascale was about; it was about power, influence, and legacy. She could live without passion and love if it meant achieving her vision of a perfect life.

When Dominic finally entered, his commanding presence filled the room effortlessly. "Dominic," she greeted warmly, rising to her feet. "I thought you wouldn't make it. How was your day?"

He greeted Vivienne with a brief peck on the cheek, murmuring an apology for his unusual lateness, having been stuck in traffic. Their conversation drifted to work and mutual acquaintances, the usual pleasantries exchanged with ease. Vivienne couldn't ignore the growing distance between them, a widening chasm that no amount of small talk could bridge. Still, she pressed on, determined to close the gap.

"Your new hire. Did they meet your expectations?"

Dominic's jaw tightened ever so slightly. "Danielle Thompson," he said, his tone deliberately neutral. A brief pause followed before he added, "She's impressive."

Vivienne's brow lifted, her intrigue piqued. "Impressive? That's high praise from you."

"She made a memorable first impression. But its early days."
Vivienne studied him intently. It was rare for Dominic to be this openly unsettled. Whoever this Danielle was, she had stirred something in him Vivienne hadn't done in years. That alone made her a threat. Silently, she filed the name away. She would find out everything there was to know about Danielle Thompson.

By dessert, Vivienne had decided to secure Dominic's attention. Leaning in slightly, she let her voice soften, laced with quiet intent. "Dominic, you know I'll always be here for you. Whatever you need." Her gaze held his, searching for a reaction.

He met her gaze, his expression unreadable. "I know, Vivienne. Thank you."

The words were polite but distant, and a familiar sting of frustration washed over her. Still, she masked it with a smile, knowing she had no choice but to hide her weakness. As they rose to leave, she clasped his hand and held on a little longer than necessary.

"Goodnight, Dominic," she huskily whispered.

"Goodnight, Vivienne," he responded, his tone cordial.

As Dominic walked away, Vivienne's mind was already at work, calculating her next move. Whether the obstacle was grief, work, or Danielle Thompson, she would eliminate it. After all, Vivienne Fox was nothing if not patient and patience always paid off.

Chapter 7

*Honour the Lord with your wealth And with the first fruits of all your crops
(income), Then your barns will be abundantly filled And your vats will overflow
with new wine.*

-Proverbs 3:9-10

The following day, Danielle eased her Range Rover out of the
driveway, the gentle purr of the engine blending with the uplifting
gospel tunes that filled the car. The sun streamed through her
windshield, bathing the quiet streets of Wanstead in a golden hue. She
loved mornings like these, serene, filled with promise, and anchored
by gratitude.

As she merged onto the main road, she reflected on how blessed
she was. Her emerald green top and tailored black pencil skirt exuded
power. She touched the wheel, her neatly manicured nails catching the
light, and smiled. Hard work marked her journey to her current
position, and each promotion was a valuable gift.

The drive into the city was smooth, her playlist alternating
between soulful hymns and vibrant praise songs that uplifted her spirit.
The music was a balm, keeping her thoughts aligned and her heart at
peace. She sang along softly, the words resonating with her: "You are
my strength when I am weak; You are the treasure that I seek."

As Danielle neared the financial district, London pulsed with
energy, the buildings towering higher, the city's rhythm quickening
around her. In the below-ground parking area of Pascale & Pascale,
she pulled into her designated spot with precision.

Stepping out, she ran a hand along the warm hood of her metallic
gold Range Rover; the sunlight catching its sleek surface. More than
just a vehicle, it was a symbol of her journey, a reward for years of

perseverance and dedication. A small smile played on her lips, but the soft ding of the elevator pulled her from her thoughts.

Adjusting her tote, she straightened her posture and strode forward, her heels clicking against the concrete floor. The gleaming Batumi Gold beauty remained behind, but the day ahead was hers to conquer.

As Danielle stepped into her office, her energy mirrored the pulse of the city outside, sharp, focused, and ready for the day ahead. Today, she would immerse herself in the company's fiscal landscape, dissecting spreadsheets and reports like uncharted maps, each figure and column holding the potential for insight. Her goal was clear: identify areas for improvement, pinpoint risks, and craft strategic solutions.

Her analytical mind was already at work, sifting through possibilities as she set her Birkin bag down and powered up her computer. The proper work was about to begin.

Danielle grinned as she thought of her tongue-in-cheek mantra: boldly go where no analyst has gone before. In truth, she relished the challenge. She enjoyed uncovering patterns in the chaos of numbers and the satisfaction of presenting insights that could drive decisions and influence outcomes. This was her wheelhouse, her passion, and she intended to make an impact.

At her previous firm, Danielle had earned a salary fitting for a Senior Financial Analyst, but not the title itself. Despite excelling in every internal assessment, she was told her tenure wasn't enough to qualify, an excuse she struggled to accept. She knew the real reason wasn't about time or capability. It was about perception.

She didn't fit their narrow mould of what a senior analyst should be. Her presence felt like an exception, not the standard, a reality that had fuelled her decision to seek a place where her expertise would be acknowledged, not questioned.

She prayed briefly for guidance, then started working. The hours flew by as she delved into data sets, dissecting financial models, and identifying potential trends. She made notes on cost-saving opportunities, flagged a few areas of concern in the budget, and began crafting a preliminary presentation for her manager.

Around mid-morning, an email from Mr Anderson, her manager, popped up in her inbox.

Subject: Follow-Up

Hi Danielle,

Great start yesterday! I've scheduled a quick one-on-one with you at 2:30 PM to discuss some ongoing projects. Advise me if there's anything particular you'd like to bring up.

Regards,
James Anderson

Danielle promptly confirmed the meeting, a small but satisfying acknowledgment that her input was valued. With renewed focus, she returned to her work, determined to enter the discussion prepared with sharp observations and actionable insights.

As she navigated a complex set of financial projections, a sense of purpose settled over her. Each challenge tackled, each milestone reached, reinforced her confidence. This, she thought, her eyes scanning the numbers with precision, is where I belong.

Shortly after, a sharp rapping sounded at the door. Before Danielle could respond, it swung open.

"Morning, Ms Thompson," Barbara announced in a clipped, nasal tone, not bothering to wait for a reply. Striding in with an air of authority, she placed a thick report on Danielle's desk.

"I need you to analyse this data and have it completed by the close of business today," she stated briskly. Her tone clarified that it was a demand, not a request.

Danielle felt irritation rising, but inhaled deeply and smiled. "Good morning, Barbara. Hope you're well and enjoying the beautiful morning. I have several reports already on my in-tray. I'll check this and finish it if possible today. If it is a priority, please log a ticket and I'll pick it up from there."

Danielle's response took Barbara aback, but she quickly composed herself. "Surely, as CFO, I do not have to request work by logging a ticket?. My word is good enough, no?" she questioned.

Danielle remained composed, offering a polite but firm response. "Your word is certainly good enough, Barbara, but for auditing purposes, your request still needs to go through the ticketing system. It's in place to protect us both." Her tone was steady and professional, leaving no room for argument while making it clear she wouldn't bypass protocol.

Barbara's smile was tight and did not reach her eyes. Inside, she was fuming, but she realised she could not push it further without arousing suspicion. "Well said, Danielle. Of course, you're right. Just testing your understanding of the system."

"I hope I passed." Danielle responded with a slight smile.

"Okay, well, I'll get this logged then," Barbara said, leaving the office. And under her breath, probably not expecting Danielle to hear, "I'm coming for you, bitch. Point one to you."

Danielle sat in stunned silence, replaying the encounter in her mind. Did she hear that correctly? Had Barbara just openly declared a vendetta? There was no point in dwelling on the pettiness. She had dealt with personalities like Barbara's before. Thinly veiled intimidation, subtle power plays, and undermining tactics dressed in forced politeness. It was a familiar game, but Danielle had no intention of playing by Barbara's rules.

It seemed she had made an enemy without even knowing why. For an instant, her mind raced, but she quickly steadied herself, whispered a prayer under her breath. "Heavenly Father, bestow upon me the wisdom and patience to navigate this situation with grace. Protect me from whatever plans she might have."

Her thoughts drifted back to a similar event at Chase and Bear. She had once agreed to complete a task for a colleague who had given her a two-day deadline. The next day, Danielle was unexpectedly called to report on the task. Fortunately, she had recovered from the shock on the spot. When Danielle later confronted Sandy, she revealed the deadline was always one day.

Sandy's betrayal had stung, but it had also been a defining lesson, one that reshaped Danielle's approach to the corporate world. It taught her that not everyone operated with integrity, and trust had to be earned, not assumed.

Anna-Mae, one of the few other ethnic minorities in the department, had given her a crucial piece of advice: always get requests in writing. It was a safeguard against ambiguity, a shield in a world where accountability often shifted like sand. That lesson had stayed with Danielle, guiding her through the cutthroat corporate environment.

Barbara's attempt to sidestep protocol felt all too familiar. Her insistence on using the ticketing system wasn't just about compliance. It was about safeguarding her position and ensuring there was a clear record of expectations.

The incident at Chase & Bear had also reinforced another crucial lesson, the value of allies. In a space where she often felt isolated, Anna-Mae had been a lifeline, offering both guidance and solidarity. Danielle knew she would need to assess her new environment carefully, and she planned to observe her colleagues more closely, noting dynamics and potential allies. She didn't need a confidante right away, but having someone she could trust, even on a purely professional level, could make all the difference.

Anna-Mae's impact on Danielle's life went far beyond office camaraderie; she had cultivated seeds of discipline and foresight in Danielle that had blossomed into a secure and thriving future. Danielle often thought of Anna-Mae as her guardian angel in those early days at Chase & Bear, her wisdom shaping not only Danielle's career but also her personal life.

Danielle could still remember the first time Anna-Mae handed her a copy of The Richest Man in Babylon.

"This isn't just a book," Anna-Mae had said, her voice steady and certain. "It's a blueprint. Follow the principles in here, and you'll never have to worry about money."

At first, Danielle had been skeptical. But as she turned the pages, the book's timeless lessons on frugality, investment, and the magic of compounding wealth drew her in. What started as curiosity quickly became a fascination that shaped her financial mindset to this day.

The wisdom didn't stop with the book. Anna-Mae had also introduced Danielle to the concept of *money pots*. A simple yet transformative way to manage finances. With each paycheck, Danielle meticulously allocated her income into designated categories: living expenses, savings, investments, education, and a small indulgence fund. It was a system that brought structure and control, ensuring that every pound had a purpose. What seemed like a small habit at first soon became the foundation of her financial independence.

This was after setting aside her 10% tithe to God. Every step she took, every financial decision she made, anchored in her deep belief that God was her ultimate provider. The 10% tithe had never been a suggestion for her; it was a commandment, a sacred practice that she embraced wholeheartedly. She understood that everything she had, her career, her home, her accomplishments, resulted from God's grace and favour.

"Discipline, Dani," Anna-Mae often said. "That's the difference between surviving and thriving. It's not about how much you make; it's about how you manage it."

By her 24th birthday, Danielle had saved enough for the down payment on her first home. A modest but charming property that marked her entry into real estate. It was a moment of pride and joy, one that she owed largely to Anna-Mae's guidance. That house had been her proof that, with the right mindset and mentors, anything was possible.

Now, years later, as she lived in her dream home in Wanstead, Danielle often reflected on Anna-Mae's teachings. They had never been just about money. They were about self-worth, empowerment, and the unwavering belief that she deserved the rewards of her hard work. Anna-Mae's lessons had shaped more than her finances; they had shaped her mindset, reminding her that financial independence was not just about wealth, but about freedom and choice.

Danielle planned to send Anna-Mae a message soon. She owed her so much more than a simple thank-you, but that would be a start. After all, Anna-Mae had not only been a mentor but also a symbol of what it meant to lift others as you climbed. In Anna-Mae's own words, *"Each one, teach one."*

For now, she would stick to her principles, document everything, and continue to excel. If Barbara wanted to make her life difficult, she'd find that Danielle was more than capable of holding her own.

Chapter 8

Let no one say when he is tempted, "I am being tempted by God" [for temptation does not originate from God, but from our own flaws]; for God cannot be tempted by [what is] evil, and He Himself tempts no one.

-James 1:13

Dominic woke up in a foul mood. To release his pent-up frustration, he went to the gym for a vigorous boxing session. Dominic's grunts echoed in the workout room as his fists collided with the heavy bag, each strike filled with frustration and confusion. Sweat dripped down his face, but he didn't stop, didn't let up. The physical exertion was the only way he could silence the warring emotions inside him.

As his punches slowed, the anger in his chest waned, replaced by an ache far more familiar: the loss of Isabella. Her name, her laughter, her voice flooded his mind. He slumped against the bag, pressing his forehead to its cool surface as memories of her enveloped him.

"Bella," he whispered, the burden of her name pressing on his heart. She had been his entire world. His partner, his confidante, his anchor. He felt a part of himself die with her. He had sworn never to let anyone else take her place, to remain faithful to her memory for as long as he lived.

Danielle's name surfaced unbidden, her image intruding into his thoughts. It wasn't just her beauty, though, that was undeniable. Her self-assurance was like a spark in the darkness he'd grown accustomed to. But what was its significance? Was he forgetting Isabella? Was he dishonouring her? The guilt clung to him like a vice, squeezing tighter with every breath.

Having stepped from the bag, Dominic paced, running a hand through his damp hair. "Get it together," he muttered. Danielle Thompson was just an employee, a talented new hire. Whatever he was feeling wasn't real. It couldn't be. It was just curiosity. Nothing more. But in his heart, he knew it wasn't simple, and it terrified him.

He walked over to the grand piano in a corner of his living room. The first notes rang out, soft and melancholic, filling the space with a haunting beauty that echoed his heartache. Dominic's fingers moved slowly, tentatively, over the keys as though the music itself might unravel him. He hadn't played this song since Isabella's passing and hadn't found the strength to relive the memories embedded in its melody. Yet now, the urge to feel close to her, even momentarily, overpowered the pain it would bring.

The melody floated, a bittersweet mix of joy and sorrow. He could almost see her sitting next to him, her slender fingers gliding over the keys with effortless grace, her laughter spilling into the silence between notes. Her presence had always been luminous, like the sun breaking through clouds, and the music had been her gift to him—a language that spoke when words were insufficient.

Dominic's breathing hitched as the song progressed, the force of his grief pressing harder with every chord. The memories came unbidden: Isabella turning to him mid-song, her eyes gleaming with mischief as she urged him to sing along;his stumbling over the lyrics; her warm embrace when he finally got it right. In that moment, her absence felt insurmountable.

As the last notes faded, the stillness in the room was deafening. Dominic sat still, his hands resting on the keys, his heart aching a fusion of longing and guilt. Playing this song had brought him closer to Isabella, but it also underscored that she was never coming back and that was all he'd have. Memories!

He squeezed his eyes shut, tilting his head back as sunlight spilled across the piano, illuminating the worn keys. A single tear escaped, sliding down his cheek. *How do I move forward when every step feels like a betrayal?*

But he knew he couldn't stay frozen in time forever. Life was pulling him forward, despite his resistance, and he was feeling the faint stirrings of something new, something terrifying and unexpected. He wasn't ready to relinquish the past; it lingered on the periphery of his heart, hoping he would to let it in. His heart in turmoil, he began his workday preparations.

Danielle walked into the quiet elevator, exhaling deeply as the doors closed, feeling the weight of the day lift. It had been a demanding one, filled with challenges and insignificant victories alike. The encounter with Barbara still played on her consciousness, as a reminder of the dynamics she would have to navigate carefully in her new role. But she was undeterred; she had dealt with worse before and knew she would emerge stronger.

As the elevator descended, she reflected on her meeting with Mr Anderson. It had been productive, with clear expectations and goals laid out for the upcoming quarter. She appreciated his leadership style, which was direct yet supportive. Still, her thoughts wandered to the peculiar absence of Barbara's ticket. Did she decide to let it go? Or is she plotting something else? Danielle knew better than to be naïve.

When the elevator doors parted to the underground car park, the cool air greeted her, a stark contrast to the warmth of the building. Danielle straightened her shoulders and adjusted her handbag, determined to end the day on a high note.

Dominic was also heading to the car park toward his waiting chauffeur. As he was about to enter his vehicle, he heard the click of heels approaching. He slowed down and glanced over his shoulder, spotting Danielle. She was so focused that she didn't notice him in her path. Dominic stayed put, curious to see when she would notice him. She almost walked straight into him before realising someone was in her way. She looked up and was stunned to see Dominic. To avoid a collision, she sidestepped, wobbled, and would have fallen had Dominic not caught her.

The touch vibrated through Danielle like an electric current. She gasped, feeling the sensation travel through her body. Dominic experienced a similar reaction; a shock of something primal coursed through him, feeling as if he had been branded. Their eyes locked, and he saw surprise in hers while she perceived the force of his gaze. She was in big trouble.

"Careful," Dominic cautioned. His hand remained a beat too long before he released her, stepping back.

"I—I'm so sorry," Danielle stammered, her cheeks warming. She retreated, regaining her composure. "I didn't see you."

A flicker of amusement, perhaps, briefly registered in Dominic's otherwise unreadable expression. He tilted his head slightly, his eyes scanning her as if trying to decipher her thoughts. "Clearly!" he said dryly, though his tone wasn't unkind. "Are you always this oblivious to your surroundings?"

She shrugged sheepishly. "Sorry, I was distracted."

Danielle straightened her posture, insistent on not letting the awkward moment unsettle her further. "Thank you for catching me. That could have ended poorly." She forced a small, professional smile, hoping to diffuse the tension.

Dominic inclined his head slightly. "You're welcome. Late night at the office?"

"Yes," she replied, adjusting her handbag strap. "Trying to create a positive impact during my first week."

"Admirable," Dominic stated, softening just a fraction. "Though you should take care not to overdo it. Balance is important."

Danielle nodded, surprised by the unexpected piece of advice. "Noted. Thank you."

"Which vehicle is yours? Come, I'll walk you," he offered.

Danielle protested, "There's no need, sir." He merely raised his eyebrows and signalled for her to walk.

Danielle made a beeline for her Range Rover, emotions swirling within her. She didn't know how she walked, still feeling the aftershocks of his touch. *My days,* she thought, *I am in big trouble.* Dominic, meanwhile, had regained his equilibrium.

"That is me. I'm thankful for your help."

Dominic's sharp eyes lingered on the opulent gold Range Rover, taking in its sleek exterior, but made no comment. Instead, his gaze returned to Danielle, unreadable yet captivatingly intense.

"Drive safely, Ms Thompson."

"Thank you, sir. You too." She unlocked her car and climbed into the driver's seat, grateful for the privacy the tinted windows offered.

Dominic watched her drive off. A slight smile tugged at his lips, quickly vanishing as he turned back toward his own vehicle.

Danielle watched Dominic through her rear-view mirror as she drove away from the car park. God, she thought, what is this? Are you testing me? Then the Holy Spirit brought a scripture to her mind: *"No temptation has overtaken you that is not common to man. God is faithful, and he will not let you be tempted beyond your ability, but with the temptation, he will also provide the way of escape, that you may be able to endure it"* (1 Corinthians 10:13). She ruminated on the scripture as she continued her journey.

Not even her ex-fiancé Carter had evoked this physical reaction in her. She and Carter met at university at the tender age of 18. He was a Christian, and they got on very well. However, once they went through marriage counselling, their views varied significantly.

She often reflected on her relationship with Carter as a turning point in her life. She had thought their shared faith and mutual respect were enough to build a marriage on. But the mandatory marriage counselling at her church had peeled back layers she hadn't envisaged.

Carter's traditional beliefs about gender roles were something she had not fully grasped during their courtship. She remembered vividly the session where he had laid out his vision for their future. He saw himself as the provider and expected her to give up her career to raise children within a year of marriage.

Danielle had felt the air leave the room as his words sunk in. She had worked diligently for her degree and had dreams of excelling in her field. The thought of abandoning that for a life that didn't align with her aspirations left her uneasy.

"But Carter," trying to reason with him during one session, "I believe God has given me these talents for a reason. I want to use them, to grow and to contribute to our family can't we support each other's dreams?"

His response had been polite but firm. "Because that's not how a family is supposed to work. A man provides and a woman nurtures. That's biblical."

Throughout the counselling process, Danielle prayed for clarity, and finally, she understood the truth: they were not meant to be. Breaking off the engagement had been one of the most difficult decisions she had made, but also the most liberating. Carter had been a good man, but not *her* man. The experience impressed upon her the significance of alignment not just in faith, but in vision, purpose and partnership. She had sworn never to compromise on that. She and Carter remained friends, corresponding occasionally.

Danielle often carried her pastor's words with her, especially when reflecting on her past engagement to Carter. His sermons, rich with wisdom and humour, always emphasised the practicalities of marriage. A topic he spoke about frequently and with deep passion. His teachings had shaped her perspective, reminding her that love alone wasn't enough; marriage required alignment, commitment, and a shared vision for the future.

He always hammered home this one point: people spent far more time preparing for the wedding than they ever did for the marriage. "A wedding is a one-day event; a marriage, however, is a lifetime commitment!" he said often.

"The problem is that people are more concerned with the aesthetics of a wedding than the substance of a marriage. You'll spend months debating whether to serve chicken or salmon, but never once discuss how you'll budget your finances together. That's why, my friends, I insist on counselling. If you can't sit down and hash out the hard stuff now, what makes you suppose you'll be capable of it when life gets messy?"

His analogy between getting a driver's license and marriage always made the congregation laugh. "You study for months to get a driving license, but for marriage? Nah, just slap on a white dress and call it a day! This is madness. No wonder so many marriages crash!" "Find someone who shares your values, yes, but also your vision. Faith is your foundation, but alignment is the structure. Without it, the house will crumble."

Today, as she balanced her career and personal life, Danielle remained steadfast in those principles. They kept her anchored, even as Dominic Pascale's presence threatened to unsettle her.

She had long understood that chemistry alone was never enough; it had to be coupled with shared values, compromise, and a commitment to grow together. Yet, despite her logic, she couldn't ignore the stark contrast between Carter and Dominic.

Carter had been warm, steady, predictable, a safe harbour. But Dominic? He was complexity wrapped in enigma, a force that awakened something raw and untested in her. And that realisation left her more conflicted than she cared to admit.

As thoughts of Dominic persisted in her mind, she reminded herself to approach any potential connection to him with caution and prayerful consideration. She wouldn't settle for anything less than the alignment her pastor had taught about so often. After all, she wasn't just preparing for a wedding day; she was committing for a lifetime to one person.

Danielle arrived home at about 11:15 p.m. Following a shower and hot chocolate, her ringing phone cut short her prayer preparations. It was her mum, Rose.

"Hi sweetie, is everything alright? While praying, the Holy Spirit prompted me to call you."

She sighed and marvelled at how God worked. "Hi Mum, I'm good, thanks. It's funny that you called. I had an experience with someone today that rattled me."

She recounted her interaction with Dominic, omitting his name and the fact that he was her boss. She did, however, mention that, her understanding was, he was not a Christian. "The Bible clearly states that an unbeliever and a believer should not be in a union, so why am I reacting this way?"

Her mum paused thoughtfully, "Perhaps you have a role to play in him giving his life to Christ? Perhaps it's a test? God works in mysterious ways, after all! Or it could be a temptation from the devil? Pray on it, sweetheart. God will guide you. Rest up. I'll see you on Sunday."

"Thanks, Mum. Love you."

Danielle dedicated the next half hour in her prayer closet and asked for divine guidance in this situation. She felt God's peace and knew that He would certainly be there for her, no matter what. Lord, lead me not into temptation, but guide me in Your will, she prayed as she climbed into bed. Her thoughts quieted, and she drifted off into a peaceful sleep.

As Danielle rested, Dominic's thoughts churned endlessly. He arrived home after the incident in the parking lot, his mind in turmoil. The encounter had left him shaken, and he couldn't stop thinking about the electric jolt he felt when he touched her hand. He went straight to his training space and started an intense boxing session, trying to punch the thoughts away, but it was no use.

Danielle Thompson kept invading his mind. Her smile, her calm presence, the way her eyes seemed to see straight through him, it all unnerved him.

He threw a last punch at the bag and sat down heavily on the bench, his chest heaving. Guilt, anger, confusion, and an undeniable attraction swirled within him. What's wrong with me? he wondered, burying his face in his hands. He had pledged never to love again after Isabella. To even entertain the idea felt like treachery.

After a long, hot shower, Dominic dressed in casual clothes and headed to the kitchen, grabbing a drink from the fridge. He stood by the window, looking towards the urban lights of Kensington, trying to make sense of the pull she had on him. He didn't know what this was or why it was happening, but Danielle was unlike anyone he had ever met.

As he drifted off to sleep, Dominic made a silent promise to himself. *I need to understand her—what drives her, what makes her tick. And maybe, just maybe, I'll find a way forward without betraying Isabella.*

Chapter 9

Whatever you do [whatever your task may be], work from the soul [that is, put in your very best effort], as [something done] for the Lord and not for men.

-Colossians 3:23

Danielle woke up the next morning feeling refreshed, the peace of her evening prayers still echoing in her soul. Her mum's words had given her much to reflect on, and she was thankful for the reminder to turn to God for guidance.

Her mum's question resurfaced in her memory. Was this a test, a mission, or a temptation? Danielle lacked the answers yet, but she trusted God to reveal His purpose in time. After a deep breath, she resolved to apply herself to her work and trust in God's plan, knowing He would guide her through any uncertainty.

She buttoned her cuffs, her stylish navy blouse and tailored trousers, making her feel confident. But it wasn't only her professional attire that gave her strength; she had also donned her spiritual armour. Ephesians 6:10-18 echoed in her mind: *"Put on the whole armour of God, that you may be able to stand against the schemes of the devil."* Navigating the corporate world and Dominic Pascale's overwhelming presence would require both strength and grace.

Her favourite gospel playlist accompanied her on her drive to work. The melodies lifted her spirits, each lyric a reminder of God's faithfulness. As the powerful words of *Way Maker* filled the car, Danielle smiled and sang along softly: *"You are here, working in this place. I worship you."* Once she reached the office, she felt grounded and ready to tackle the day.

Around mid-morning, as Danielle settled into her tasks, a notification popped up on her computer, a ticket request from Barbara, just as she had advised.

A small smile tugged at her lips. So, she listened. Danielle appreciated the adherence to protocol, even if it was begrudging. It was a small but meaningful victory, proving that professionalism would always outweigh power plays.

Dominic stood outside Danielle's office, his hand hovering over the doorframe. Why am I even here? He hadn't planned to visit her, but after their interaction at the parking lot last night, she had lingered in his thoughts far longer than he cared to admit.

His hesitation frustrated him. He had faced hostile boardrooms, negotiated multi-million-pound deals, and managed crises without flinching. Yet here he was, standing outside her door like a schoolboy, debating whether to knock. Before he could talk himself out of it, he rapped lightly on the door.

The sudden knock jolted Danielle from her deep focus on the intricate financial analysis. She blinked, momentarily pulled from the maze of numbers.

"Come in," she called, glancing up, curiosity flickering across her face.

Dominic opened the door, his presence immediately filling her office. Dressed impeccably in a baby-blue shirt that emphasised his broad shoulders, paired with navy trousers and a slim black tie. The subtle scent of his cologne reached her before his words did.

"Good morning, Ms Thompson," he began, his voice calm but authoritative. "I wanted to discuss the financial projections for the next quarter. Your analysis will be crucial in shaping our strategic planning."

Danielle straightened, willing her pulse to steady. "Of course, Mr Pascale. Please, have a seat," she said, gesturing to the chair opposite her desk.

As Dominic settled into the chair, he leaned forward slightly, his piercing gaze locking onto hers. Danielle felt the intensity of his presence, but she refused to let it unsettle her. "I've been reviewing the preliminary figures, but I want to ensure we're not missing any opportunities—or risks. I trust your expertise in this."

Danielle nodded and turned to her computer, pulling up the relevant documents. "I've already started analysing the data." "Let me walk you through my initial findings."

As she spoke, Dominic listened intently, his attention riveted on her face. Her thoroughness and clarity impressed him. Her insights were sharp, her approach meticulous. He admired her professionalism, even as a piece of him remained distracted by her presence.

"Excellent work, Ms Thompson," he commented when she concluded. "Your insights are invaluable. I appreciate your hard work and dedication."

Danielle offered a polite smile. "I'm happy to contribute to the company's success." Her tone was professional yet warm, carrying the quiet confidence that had become her signature.

As Dominic stood to leave, his eyes scanned over her, lingering for a moment. He noticed the matching shades of their outfits and his eyes twinkled with amusement. "Well, I guess we've officially entered the synchronised wardrobe phase."

Danielle glanced down at her navy ensemble, then back up at him. A faint blush crept up her cheeks, but she maintained a playful tone. "It appears so."

"Great minds," he grinned. "Perhaps it's a sign."

Danielle arched an eyebrow. "Or perhaps it's just a coincidence," she said smoothly.

Dominic chuckled. "Guess we'll never know." He hesitated. "Should you require anything, Ms Thompson, my door is always open."

"I appreciate it, Mr Pascale," Danielle replied, her heart racing as the door closed behind him.

Dominic walked back to his office, his thoughts in turmoil. He couldn't resist the growing attraction he felt for Danielle. She intrigued him, not just professionally, but personally. He needed to proceed cautiously. Allowing personal feelings to cloud his judgment was a luxury he couldn't afford, not as the head of Pascale & Pascale.

Danielle, meanwhile, sat at her desk, trying to refocus. But her interaction with Dominic lingered in her mind. His words, his demeanour, even the playful banter, all of it felt significant, so she couldn't quite explain.

As the clock approached lunchtime, Danielle cleared her head. She grabbed her lunch and walked to a nearby park, the sunshine a welcome reprieve from the office's fluorescent lights. On a bench beneath a tree canopy, she basked in the sun's warmth, silently praying for clarity and strength. Whatever was unfolding with Dominic Pascale, she was certain of one thing: she would face it with faith and resolve.

Chapter 10

For wherever there is jealousy (envy) and contention (rivalry and selfish ambition), there will also be confusion (unrest, disharmony, rebellion) and all sorts of evil and vile practices.

-James 3:16

The 14th floor buzzed with speculation and curiosity. Danielle and Dominic's unexpected encounter had sent ripples through the office, sparking quiet conversations and knowing glances. Employees exchanged theories and observations, their whispers weaving through the usual hum of productivity. Something about the interaction had caught their attention—and no one was ignoring it.

"Did you see Mr Pascale up on the fourteenth floor today? That never happens," one colleague murmured by the coffee machine.

"And he spent nearly an hour in her office! What could they possibly be discussing?" came the curious reply.

While most were intrigued, Barbara Johnson's anger burned. Danielle's presence threatened Barbara's long-standing position as the centre of attention and influence. She gloried in being the office star, the one everyone admired and talked about. Losing that spotlight was not an option. In her office, Barbara paced, her thoughts swirling with plans to regain control. "This is unacceptable. She's only been here a few days, and already she's causing a stir. I need to act fast."

Barbara devised a strategy—subtle sabotage. She would plant seeds of doubt, casting Danielle as overly ambitious, inexperienced, or disruptive. The key was to be discreet, to let the whispers do the damage without ever appearing responsible.

Her first move? Gathering allies.

That evening, she invited a few trusted confidants for drinks, carefully weaving a narrative. Danielle was an outsider, stepping on toes, disrupting the balance. A little exaggeration here, a vague insinuation there. By the next morning, the office gossip mill was already in motion, and suspicions about Danielle had taken root.

Dominic told himself that visiting Danielle's office was purely professional, a necessary step to discuss the company's financial projections. Yet, no matter how much he tried to rationalise it, he couldn't ignore the undercurrent of personal interest pulling him in.

His thoughts drifted to her more often than he cared to admit, replaying their brief yet charged interactions. There was an undeniable spark between them, one that unsettled him. Was he crossing a line, allowing personal feelings to bleed into professional decisions? The question lingered, but he wasn't sure he wanted to face the answer.

Barbara's plans to undermine Danielle set the stage for a confrontation. Danielle, unknowingly caught in the crossfire, continued to work diligently, unaware of the challenges that lay ahead. And Dominic, torn between his responsibilities and his growing attraction to Danielle, found himself at a crossroads, unsure of the right path to take.

By Friday afternoon, Danielle experienced a feeling of accomplishment. The week had been demanding, but she had tackled her responsibilities with determination. At precisely 4:00 p.m, the sound of someone knocking broke her focus.

"Hi, Danielle," Emily greeted warmly. "A few of us are heading to Bar 11 for drinks. Want to join?"

Danielle tilted her head, confused. "At 4:00 p.m.?"

Emily chuckled. "It's tradition here. Fridays, we clock out early for some downtime."

"Good to know," Danielle remarked with a smile. "Thanks for the invite, but I will pass."

"Sure," Emily said, her smile faltered slightly. "If you change your mind, you know where to find us. Have a great weekend, and it's been lovely working with you this week."

"Likewise, Emily. Thanks for all your help," Danielle replied, watching her leave. She appreciated the gesture, but preferred to unwind her own way.

Emily softly shut the door and thought, oh well, it was worth a try. She really liked Danielle, who was such a lovely and genuine person and always had a beautiful smile and a good word. Certainly not pompous as Barbara. Emily invited Danielle because she heard the things that were being said about her and wanted people to see Danielle as she did.

Danielle watched Emily leave, feeling a mixture of relief and a hint of regret. She appreciated the invitation, but bars were not her scene.

At Bar 11, Emily joined her colleagues, experiencing a twinge of disappointment. She had hoped Danielle would come along, not just to bond, but to dispel the growing rumours.

"She's not coming," Emily said, sliding onto a barstool next to Karen.

"Of course not," Karen scoffed. "Probably off with Mr Pascale again. I heard he remained in her office for an hour the other day."

Emily frowned. "That's not fair, Karen. You don't know that."

Karen shrugged, a smirk on her face. "Just saying what everyone's thinking. Less than a week here, and she's already caught his eye? Makes you wonder."

Emily sighed, recognising the uphill battle ahead in countering the growing gossip. The office chatter had taken on a life of its own, and trying to extinguish it felt like chasing smoke.

Rather than fuel the toxicity brewing around Danielle, she chose a different approach. With a practiced smile, she smoothly shifted the conversation, steering it toward safer, more productive ground, anything to avoid getting entangled in the web of office politics.

Danielle packed up her belongings, reflecting on the week. It was a flurry of unfamiliar faces and responsibilities. The lingering tension from her interaction with Dominic had receded as she focused on her work. Right as she was prepared to leave, another knock came at her door.

"Enter," she called, slightly exasperated.

Mr Anderson appeared, his demeanour hesitant. "Hi, Ms Thompson. I simply wanted to say you've done excellent work this week. Keep it up."

Danielle offered a warm smile. "Thank you, Mr Anderson."

He hesitated. "Just a word of advice. Be mindful of maintaining boundaries."

Danielle blinked, surprised. "I beg your pardon? What boundaries have I crossed?"

Mr Anderson shifted uncomfortably. "There's been some chatter about Mr Pascale's visit to your office earlier this week. Just thought I'd give you a heads-up."

"Chatter?" Danielle asked, incredulous. "It was a work meeting. What's there to talk about?"

Mr Anderson gave a half-shrug. "Office dynamics can be tricky. Just be careful. Have a good weekend."

He exited quickly, leaving Danielle stunned. She stood in her office, trying to process what had just happened. Gossip about her and Dominic? How absurd!

With a deep breath, she decided she would address it head-on Monday. For now, she grabbed her bag and left the office, ready to unwind after an eventful week.

Chapter 11

A cheerful heart is a good medicine, but a downcast spirit dries up the bones.

-Proverbs 17:22

Danielle heaved a long sigh as she closed her prayer room door behind her, the serenity of the space lingering in her heart. The pressure of the week, the gossip, a renewed sense of clarity replaced the tension. She prompted herself to leave it all in God's hands, trusting in His timing and guidance.

Rejuvenated, she picked up her phone. If anyone could lift her spirits higher, it was Ten.

The phone rang twice before Ten's cheerful voice answered. "Hey, Dani! What's up?"

"Hey, Ten! I'm good. I need some company this morning. Are you free for coffee?"

"Absolutely! I was just thinking about you. Usual spot in an hour?"

"Perfect. See you then."

After hanging up, Danielle smiled, already feeling lighter. She dressed in a comfortable yet chic outfit, grabbed her keys and headed to their favourite café. An hour later, Danielle stepped into the warm, inviting café, the rich aroma of fresh coffee wrapping around her like a hug. She spotted Ten right away, waving from a window seat, two steaming cups already on the table.

"There she is!" Ten called, her face lighting up. "Looking fabulous, as always."

Danielle laughed and hugged her friend before she sat down. "You're too kind, Ten. You're glowing today too!"

"Alright, Dani, spill. I can tell something's on your mind."

Danielle hesitated for a moment before diving in. She recounted her week, the unexpected challenges, the whispers circulating around the office, and the subtle but undeniable tension with Dominic. Though she remained composed, speaking about it aloud made it all feel more real, the complexities of her new role unfolding in ways she hadn't expected.

Ten paid close attention. "Office politics, the worst. But you've handled it like a champ, Dani. You've always been strong, and your faith is your superpower. Don't forget that."

"Thanks, Ten," Danielle said, feeling a wave of gratitude. "I guess I just needed to vent. It's been a lot, but I'm trying to avoid letting it get to me."

"And you're not alone in this," Ten said firmly. "If anyone tries to mess with you, they'll have to deal with me first." Her exaggerated bravado made Danielle laugh, the tension melting away.

They spent the next hour catching up on lighter topics, swapping stories, and laughing over their favourite inside jokes. The conversation flowed effortlessly, a welcome escape from the pressures of work. By the time they parted, Danielle felt refreshed, grounded, and ready to take on whatever challenges lay ahead.

That afternoon, she visited her mother's house, where the familiar, comforting aroma of stewed chicken and rice greeted her the moment she stepped inside. Home. No matter how demanding life became, this was where she always found peace.

"Hi, Mum!"

Rose appeared from the kitchen, wiping her hands on a dish towel. "There's my girl! Come on in, I've just made your favourite."

Danielle enveloped her mother in a tender embrace. "You always know exactly what I need."

Rose offered her a meaningful look. "That's what mothers are for. Now, let's sit down and chat."

They sat at the kitchen table, the comforted meal filling Danielle with warmth. "So, how's the new job going, sweetheart?" Rose asked, eyeing her daughter carefully.

Danielle sighed, setting down her fork. "It's been a mixed bag. I love the work, but there's this woman, Barbara. She's making things difficult. It feels like she's trying to undermine me at every turn."

Rose's brow furrowed. "Oh, Danielle, that's tough. Do you think she feels threatened by you?"

"Maybe," Danielle admitted. "She's been there a while, and I'm new. But it's not just that. It's like she's looking for reasons to push my buttons. Staying professional is exhausting some days."

Rose extended her hand across the table, squeezing Danielle's hand. "People often judge what they don't understand. Maybe she sees your potential, and it scares her."

Danielle nodded slowly. "I only hope to do my job and not get pulled into office drama. And then there's Dominic..."

"Dominic, well do tell?"

Danielle chuckled, feeling a little self-conscious. "He's complicated. We work together, and there's definitely chemistry. But he's got walls up. And I don't even know where he stands with his faith."

Rose gave her daughter a thoughtful smile. "Sounds like you've got much to handle, honey. Remember, stay true to yourself. Let God guide your steps, even in the murky waters. A prayer or two for Barbara and Dominic wouldn't hurt either."

Danielle laughed, feeling lighter. "You're right, mum. Thank you."

Danielle left her mother's house feeling both comforted and strengthened by the wisdom her mother had imparted. Her mum's words resonated as she as she drove home, the familiar scripture from Ephesians grounding her thoughts. The reminder that her struggles weren't merely with the people around her, but with darker spiritual forces, gave her a new perspective.

Her mother was always a pillar of faith and wisdom in her life, and her advice to stay "prayed up" resounded deeply. This served as a reminder that Danielle needed to lean even more on her spiritual foundation, especially when faced with challenges that seemed to arise out of nowhere.

As she drove past the silent houses, Danielle reflected on the occurrences of the past week. The strange encounter with Dominic, the gossip at the office and the tension with Barbara all seemed to stem from something bigger that she couldn't quite put her finger on yet. But her mother's words gave her peace. Danielle knew that if she remained faithful and trusted in God, the truth would come to light in His timing.

When Danielle arrived home, she went straight to her place of worship, feeling the need for quiet reflection. She understood she could not control the actions or thoughts of others, but she could choose her response. As she settled onto her knees, the words of Matthew 5:44, *"pray for those who persecute you,"* lingered in her heart. After a deep breath, she began praying for her coworkers, especially those who might have ill intentions.

She asked God to bring any hidden agendas to light, to guide her steps and to grant her wisdom and grace in her interactions, finding comfort, choosing faith over frustration and relinquishing the need to control what was beyond her power.

Chapter 12

"O come, let us worship and bow down: let us kneel before the LORD our maker."

-Psalms 95:6

Sunday morning dawned with a golden glow filtering through Danielle's window, promising a beautiful day ahead. She woke early, as always, spending her first moments in her prayer room. The tranquillity of the environment wrapped around her as she sought guidance and strength, her prayers pouring out with sincerity. What transpired this week had left her feeling unanchored, but she trusted that God's plan would unfold in His perfect timing.

After a light breakfast, Danielle dressed in a calf-length lilac dress and travelled to church. The moment she stepped through the doors, serenity washed over her. Familiar faces lit up as they greeted her warmly, exchanging smiles and kind words.

This was her church family, people she had shared countless Sundays with, a steadfast source of encouragement and fellowship. With the choir rehearsing in the background and the delicate scent of fresh lilies in the air, she was reminded of why this place always felt like home.

The service began with uplifting worship and Danielle found herself lost in the music, singing praises to God with all her heart.

The sermon that day was powerful, focusing on the importance of unwavering trust in God, especially in life's most challenging circumstances. Pastor Ike began by reading from Proverbs 3:5-6: *"Trust in the Lord with all your heart, and lean not on your own understanding; in all your ways acknowledge Him, and He shall direct your paths."* He explained that our understanding is limited, but God's wisdom is infinite and therefore, we must trust His guidance, even when our situation seems unclear or discouraging.

The second scripture came from Romans 8:28: *"And we know that all things work together for good to those who love God, to those who are called according to His purpose."* He emphasised that God's plan for us doesn't eliminate hardships but assures us that every trial, every delay and every disappointment is part of a larger tapestry being woven for our benefit and His glory.

He reminded the congregation that while Joseph suffered betrayal, slavery and imprisonment, God used those experiences to position him to save a nation (Genesis 50:20). "God's plans are always for our good, even when they're wrapped in adversity."

As he spoke, Danielle reflected on her own life. The message resonated deeply with her, reinforcing the advice her mother had imparted to her the day before. Her mom had reminded her that trusting God sometimes means waiting, even when we want immediate answers.

He ended with a call to release anxiety, holding fast to Philippians 4:6-7: *"Be anxious for nothing, but in everything by prayer and supplication, with thanksgiving, let your requests be made known to God; and the peace of God, which surpasses all understanding, will guard your hearts and minds through Christ Jesus."*

Danielle left the service feeling renewed. The sermon strengthened her faith and reminded her she could entrust her fears and uncertainties to a God who sees and knows all.

Following the service, Danielle chatted with friends. They shared laughs, discussed recent events in each other's lives, and spoke about the sermon. The fellowship was exactly what Danielle needed, reminding her she was not alone on her journey. She had a powerful community of believers who supported and loved her.

While Danielle sought solace at church, Dominic was immersed in his own weekend routine, trying to distract himself with work. By

Saturday evening, however, he craved a change of pace and met up with his old friend Daze, someone who had been an important part of his life despite coming from a vastly unique background.

Daze was a force to be reckoned with, shaped by a life that had tested him at every turn. Born into hardship, he had endured the kind of struggles that Dominic could barely fathom. His mother's battle with addiction ended tragically when he was just 19, leaving him to navigate adulthood without her guidance. His father's incarceration a decade earlier, at only nine, had thrust him into a world where survival depended on grit and determination.

Despite the odds, Daze had defied every expectation. Through sheer willpower and relentless hustle, he built a portfolio of successful businesses, amassing wealth and respect in his own right. His journey was anything but conventional and Dominic's father had always disapproved of their friendship, viewing Daze as a liability.

But Dominic saw past the prejudice. Daze's raw authenticity, unyielding resilience and unshakable loyalty were qualities that Dominic admired deeply. Over the years, their bond had grown unbreakable, more akin to brothers than friends.

"Man, it's been way too long since you came by," Daze greeted him. "I thought you were stuck in your office."

"You understand, Daze. Business doesn't stop. But it's good to kick back for a change."

Daze leaned back in his plush leather chair, sipping his whiskey. The city skyline glittered through the large windows of his penthouse.

"True, true. So, what's new? And don't give me the usual work's busy. I want something real."

Dominic chuckled, "When have I ever been anything but real with you?"

"Bro, you keep your cards so close to your chest, I'm surprised you don't have paper cuts. Spill it."

Dominic hesitated, staring into his glass, debating whether to bring her up. Then, before he could stop himself, the words came out.

"There's someone at work...Danielle."

Daze's eyebrows shot up in disbelief. "Wait, are you serious? The Dominic Pascale is actually mentioning a woman? This is big."

"Don't start."

"Oh, I'm starting. Let me get comfortable for this," said Daze, sitting up and grinning. "Alright, go on. What's the deal with this, Danielle?"

Dominic gathered his thoughts.

"It's hard to explain. She's not like anyone I've met before. She's sharp, confident and grounded. And yet, she stirs something in me. Something I haven't felt since..."

He trailed off, the name he didn't need to say lingering between them.

"Since Isabella." Daze filled in.

Dominic nodded, a pained look crossing his face.

"Yeah. And I feel guilty for even thinking about someone else. From the first day she walked into that boardroom, she stirred something within me."

"Like she's calling you out without calling you out?"

Dominic laughed lightly, "Exactly."

Daze studied his brother, his grin fading into something more thoughtful.

"Look, Dom. You've been carrying Isabella's memory like it's a ball and chain. And don't get me wrong, I get it. She was one-of-a-kind. But maybe this Danielle could be your way forward?"

Dominic frowned, processing the words.

"It feels too soon."

"It's been 18 months, man. You're allowed to feel something again. The question is, are you brave enough to let yourself?"

Dominic didn't answer right away. Instead, he imbibed his whiskey, staring out at the lights of the city, Danielle's image playing in his mind.

Daze was thrilled a grin spreading across his face. "Dom, this is big," he said. You should follow this. See where it goes. Don't be afraid."

"It would be inappropriate, D. I barely know her and she's my employee. I don't wish to cross any lines."

Daze laughed, dismissing his concerns with a wave of his hand. "Man, you're just making excuses. Life's too short to let opportunities pass you by. At least, if nothing else, it'll get Vivienne to back off."

On Sunday, Dominic visited his mother, as was his and Daze's custom, enjoying the warm summer breeze and the scent of blooming roses. His mother was perceptive and had always read him like a book. When he mentioned Danielle, his eyes revealed interest.

"She sounds lovely. I'd like to meet her someday."

"Mum, I hardly know anything about her beyond what's on her CV," Dominic replied, keeping his tone neutral, trying to downplay his interest.

Then, as if to shift the focus, he added, "What about Vivienne?"

His mother reached over and patted his hand. "I know how you feel about Vivienne. She's a friend, nothing more. I wish you happiness, son, with whomever you choose. After Isabella, I didn't think I would ever see that light in your eyes again. Please don't let it go."

Dominic looked at his mother, the woman who consistently stood by him, and felt a deep sense of gratitude. She had always supported him, even when she disagreed with his choices. Her words stayed with him as he drove home, a quiet steadfastness settling in his heart. As the sun sank below the horizon, Dominic stood by his window, staring at the city lights. His thoughts were a tangle of guilt, hope, and curiosity. Daze and his mother were right. He'd been holding back for too long. He permitted himself to consider the possibility of moving on.

One step at a time, he thought, a quiet firmness settling over him. No matter what the future brought, he wouldn't let fear dictate his path.

Chapter 13

And if he sins against you seven times in a day and seven times, he returned to you said, 'I repent,' you must forgive him."

-Luke 17:4

On Monday morning, Danielle followed her usual routine, dressing in her sharpest outfit and arming herself with a prayer for wisdom and strength. The whispers and stares followed her like an unwelcome shadow. The buzz of speculation seemed to stick to the walls, thickening the air as she proceeded to her office. Her back straightened with each step. *They can talk,* she told herself. *God sees my heart, and I won't let their words define me.*

She stood for a moment, straightening the papers on her desk as though organising her thoughts. *Stay prayed up and trust God to reveal the truth in His time.* She pulled her chair closer to her desk and dived into her work, determined to let her actions speak louder than the whispers beyond her door.

Meanwhile, Dominic sat at his desk, his fingers drumming a steady beat against the polished wood. Across from him, Andre shifted uncomfortably, his unease palpable.

"Sir," Andre began hesitantly, choosing his words carefully. "There's chatter around the office about your visit to Ms Thompson's office."

Dominic's gaze sharpened instantly. "And what exactly are they saying?"

Andre hesitated, glancing down briefly before forcing himself to meet Dominic's eyes. "They're implying that it wasn't strictly professional."

A muscle tightened in Dominic's jaw, but his face remained stoic. "Interesting," he said evenly. "And this gossip, does it affect our financial projections? Our bottom line?"

Andre blinked, startled. "No, sir."

"Then let them talk," Dominic replied, his voice as cold as steel. "But keep me informed if their distractions affect their work."

As Andre left, Dominic's controlled demeanour faltered. He stood and paced to the window, his reflection blending with the London skyline. The rumours didn't bother him for his own sake, but that Danielle's reputation was at stake sparked a frustration he couldn't ignore. She didn't deserve this.

His visit to her office had been professional, he had convinced himself. But now he couldn't refute the growing complexity of his feelings. Danielle Thompson wasn't just another employee; she was a presence that unsettled and intrigued him in equal measure.

Fix it, Pascale, he thought. But how? Any public action would only fuel the rumours. No, this required discretion. He would call her later, away from the watchful eyes of the office.

That evening, Danielle was curled up in her reading nook when her mobile rang, an unknown number flashing on her screen. "Hello?"

"Hi, Danielle. This is Dominic."

Her heart fluttered. "Mr Pascale?" she answered, unable to hide her surprise.

"Yes, and I'm sorry to bother you. I wanted to apologise."

"Apologise for what?"

"For the situation my visit caused. I didn't intend to put you in such a position.

"Mr Pascale," she began, but he interrupted.

"Dominic," he corrected gently. "Please, call me Dominic. We're not at the workplace."

The informality startled her. She hesitated, choosing her words carefully. "I prefer to keep things professional. It avoids unnecessary misunderstandings, especially considering the situation."

Dominic admired her composure, though it frustrated him. She was drawing a line, one he wasn't used to encountering. "Fair enough." "I just wanted you to know that I didn't intend to cause you distress."

"Thank you, but there's no need to apologise. People will talk and then they'll move on to something else."

"I hear that, but if you ever feel overwhelmed, you can call or text me anytime." I'll text you my number."

The offer took Danielle aback. She doubted she would ever use it, but that he gave her direct access to him was interesting. "I'll keep that in mind," she said politely. "Thanks again for the call. I appreciate it."

"Goodnight, Danielle."

She set the book down with a sigh, staring into the distance, and replayed the conversation in her head, frowning slightly. His request for first names made her pause. It was subtle but significant, a blurring of professional boundaries that left her perplexed.

Danielle wasn't sure if Dominic was an enemy, however she realised she needed to tread carefully. Although her heart pulled her in one direction, her mind and spirit remained firmly rooted in her faith. She would continue to depend on God's guidance, knowing that He would reveal the path she should take.

Determined to refocus, she shook her head and grabbed her book again. Just a moment of distraction, she reassured herself sternly. Stick to your principles, Danielle. Resolutely, she returned her to the story, letting the words on the page draw her away from the unsettling thoughts.

Across the city, Dominic laced up his sneakers and headed to his home gym. The steady rhythm of his punches against the heavy bag did little to quiet his thoughts.

Danielle affected him. He wanted to peel back the layers, to learn what lay beneath her composed exterior. But he knew the risks. Office gossip had already begun swirling and any move he made could have repercussions not just for her, but for him as well. With a shake of his head, Dominic landed a solid punch on the heavy bag. Control yourself, Pascale, he thought.

As the city settled into quiet, two souls wrestled with their thoughts. Danielle clung to her faith, asking for guidance amidst confusion. Dominic confronted emotions he thought he had buried, wondering if he was prepared to take a step into the unknown. The night stretched on, their worlds separated by distance but connected by an unspoken thread. And as they drifted to sleep, their paths seemed destined to cross again, each carrying the burden of their own uncertainties.

Chapter 14

Therefore, whatever you have said in the dark shall be heard in the light and what you have whispered in private rooms shall be proclaimed on the housetops.

-Luke 12:3

Danielle had settled into her routine with a quiet but unwavering determination. Long hours and intense focus were nothing new. She had spent years refining the discipline it took to thrive in high-powered corporate spaces. But as an ethnic minority in a world where expectations often felt heavier, she knew her success wasn't just about personal achievement. It was about representation, about proving again and again, that she belonged.

She bore the weight with grace, even when it kept her at her desk long after the office had emptied. Early mornings and late nights were second nature, ingrained in her through years of striving not just for excellence, but to be undeniable. Her meticulous work quickly earned her a reputation for precision, reliability, and sharp insight. A professional force to be reckoned with.

But with praise came whispers. Speculation about her interactions with Dominic Pascale followed her down hallways, lurking in the break rooms and boardrooms alike. Outwardly, Danielle dismissed the gossip, refusing to let it shake her focus. But inwardly? It gnawed at her, an irritation she couldn't quite shake. She had worked too hard to be reduced to office rumours.

That week, she was involved in a complex project involving cross-departmental coordination across multiple time zones. The challenge invigorated her, but it also demanded every ounce of her focus. Quick breaks on the office sofa and cups of coffee fuelled her as she pushed through the mounting workload.

By Thursday evening, fatigue was creeping in, though Danielle pressed on. The ring of her desk phone suddenly interrupted the quiet hum of her office.

"Danielle, it's Dominic," his unmistakable voice came through the line, low, steady, and authoritative. "How's the project progressing?"

There was no small talk, no unnecessary pleasantries, just direct, to the point. Classic Dominic Pascale.

"Good evening, Mr Pascale. I'm making solid headway. Is there something specific you'd like to discuss?"

"Let's discuss over dinner," he said without hesitation. "I've booked a private room at The Rubix for 9:00 p.m."

Danielle blinked, surprised. "That's unnecessary, Mr Pascale," she replied, keeping her tone polite but firm.

"Danielle, this isn't a request. I'm travelling tomorrow unexpectedly, and we need to complete some details. Since I already have the reservation, it makes sense to use the time productively." "Besides, I'm famished," he said in a lighter tone.

The unexpected shift in Dominic's tone left Danielle momentarily speechless. She weighed her options carefully. Realistically, declining wasn't an option. But the setting he suggested set off quiet alarms in her mind. Still, her professionalism prevailed, or at least, that's what she told herself.

"Alright," she exhaled softly. "I'll see you there at 9:00."

"Perfect. See you then," he said before hanging up.

Keep it professional, she resolutely instructed herself. Still, she understood the negative visual impact of the situation. What she least needed was to provide more fodder for the office rumour mill. But with her stomach growling, a sharp reminder that her last meal had been a rushed sandwich hours ago. She resolved to approach the evening with her usual poise.

Having checked the time, she realised she had just enough time to freshen up. She entered the shower in her office, washing off the fatigue of the day before, changing into the spare clothes she kept on hand: a pair of tailored slacks and a semi-formal blouse. Simple and understated, the outfit struck a harmonious blend of professionalism and comfort. She tied her hair into a bun, adding a touch of mascara and lip gloss to complete the look. With one last glance in the mirror, she had a hunch that tonight's event might hold more importance than usual. Stay focused, Danielle. This is business, nothing more.

Danielle arrived at The Rubix promptly at 9:00 p.m., stepping into a world of understated elegance. The discreet side entrance, the muted hum of private conversations, and the soft glow of ambient lighting all exuded an air of exclusivity.

She followed the manager down a plush, carpeted hallway, each step deepening the quiet intrigue and unease building within her. Whatever this meeting was, Dominic had gone to great lengths to ensure privacy.

Rather than meeting in the premier restaurant, he had arranged for a secluded setting, away from prying eyes and potential gossip. It was thoughtful, calculated, exactly what she would expect from him. And yet, that knowledge didn't quiet the tension coiling in her chest.

When the manager accessed the private room, Danielle's breath caught for a moment. Dominic stood as she entered, his tall frame silhouetted against the warm light of the room. He dressed casually, but even in a simple shirt and slacks, he exuded an air of authority. A small, elegantly set table awaited them, fragrance of fresh blooms awaited them, the scent of fresh flowers mingling with the faint aroma of rich wood polish. The scene was intimate, yet carefully orchestrated, reinforcing the professional context of their meeting.

"Good evening, Danielle," Dominic said, his voice smooth yet unmistakably intent.

As his gaze settled on her, something shifted. The usual professional detachment wavered, giving way to something warmer, something unguarded. For a fleeting moment, the ever-composed Dominic Pascale was simply a man, not a CEO.

"You look beautiful."

The words came quietly, almost as if he hadn't meant to say them aloud. But now that they were out, he didn't take them back. The words lingered in the air, unexpected and disarming.

Danielle felt a flutter in her chest, but quickly steeled herself. "Thank you, Mr Pascale."

"Dominic," he corrected smoothly, a hint of a smile playing at his lips. "We're not in the office right now. I'd prefer if you addressed me by my first name in private."

Danielle hesitated, the request feeling oddly intimate. She wasn't sure if it was the setting, the warmth in his voice, or the way his gaze held hers, but something about it made her pause.

"Thank you, Dominic," she repeated, her tone measured but polite. The name felt unfamiliar on her tongue, yet undeniably significant.

He indicated for her to sit, pulling out her chair with practiced ease.

"I hope the escort was convenient."

"It was," she replied, glancing around the room. "This is a beautiful setting."

"I wanted to ensure we could have an uninterrupted conversation."

The conversation shifted to ordering dinner, a welcome reprieve that eased some of the underlying tension. With their selections made and the menus set aside, Dominic leaned forward slightly, his expression tinged with curiosity.

"So, Danielle," he mused, his tone lighter now, "what do you do when you're not revolutionising our financial strategies?"

There was something disarmingly genuine in the way he asked, an interest that felt more personal than professional.

Danielle smiled, folding her hands on the table. "Well, my faith is very important to me. I'm involved in a few ministry groups at church and love spending time in nature—hiking, mostly. It helps me recharge."

"Church and hiking, that's a combination I don't hear often. Does it ever conflict with your work?"

"Sometimes," she admitted. "But it keeps me grounded. It's easy to become engrossed in everything and lose sight of what matters." She inclined her head slightly. "What about you? What's your escape?"

Dominic chuckled, glancing down at his hands. "The gym, mostly. It's a way to burn off stress. But beyond that, I suppose I have thought little about it lately."

Danielle's expression softened as she studied him for a moment. "You seem like someone who carries many burdens on your shoulders," she said gently. Then, with a small, knowing smile, she added, "Maybe you should."

Her words hung between them, a quiet challenge wrapped in sincerity. Dominic, for all his composure, wasn't used to being seen this way, as someone who might need a moment to breathe, to let go.

"Maybe I should," Dominic admitted. There was something about her words, unexpected yet strikingly perceptive.

Shifting the conversation, he leaned back slightly, a hint of curiosity in his tone. "What else do you do besides church and hiking?"

Danielle's eyes sparkled as she continued. "I love reading, too. There's something about getting lost in a good book that's like an adventure of its own, you know? And dancing," she said with a shy laugh. "I'm not a professional, but when I'm home alone, I'll put on some music and just lose myself. It's liberating."

Dominic's intrigue grew. "Reading, I can understand. Dancing? It's hard to imagine you letting loose like that."

She laughed, leaning back slightly. "Everyone needs a release, and when you're alone, it's easy to just be. No one watching, no judgments."

He nodded, feeling a sense of admiration. "It's refreshing to hear someone talk about the simple things. Sometimes, I've forgotten how to just be myself."

Their food arrived, putting a pause to the conversation. Danielle hummed softly as she took her first bite, a small sound of appreciation that made Dominic pause mid-bite, sending a shiver down his spine. It was such an unguarded moment, a view of her as more than the composed professional he saw daily. He watched her, captivated by her ease and genuineness.

Danielle looked up, realising he had stopped eating. "Are you alright?" she questioned.

"Yes, I'm fine," Dominic quickly resumed his meal. But his mind raced. How was it that something so unassuming could leave him so unsteady? Her soft hums of contentment was disarming and driving him to the edge of his self-control.

Their conversation flowed naturally, gradually shifting toward work. Danielle detailed the challenges of coordinating the project across multiple time zones, her insights sharp and methodical. She spoke with precision, outlining obstacles and solutions with the ease of someone who had done the work, not just understood it. Dominic listened intently, his respect for her growing with every word.

"I appreciate the effort you're putting into this," he said sincerely, his tone carrying an unmistakable note of acknowledgment. "It's difficult, especially with the long hours you've been keeping."

It wasn't just praise; it was recognition. And coming from Dominic Pascale, that meant something. "Thanks," Danielle responded. "I simply want to make sure everything is perfect."

"You've done more than that. Your leadership has set a tone for the team. It's rare to see someone command respect so effortlessly."

Danielle felt a slight warmth creep into her cheeks at Dominic's unexpected compliment, but she quickly redirected the conversation, focusing on the project's next steps. Her tone remained composed, professional, determined to keep things on track. The shift helped dissipate some of the tension, grounding them back in familiar territory.

As the evening wound down, Dominic offered to arrange a car for her. Danielle initially resisted, but his insistence won out. He offered his hand as he stood by the car door. "I appreciate your time tonight, Danielle."

She grasped his hand, the brief contact sending a shiver through both of them. "Goodnight, Dominic." she slipped into the car. Once the door closed, she instinctively looked back and saw him staring at her.

Dominic watched as the car disappeared into the night, his thoughts a torrent of emotions he wasn't ready to name.

Chapter 15

Anxiety weighs down the human heart, but a good word cheers it up.

-Proverbs 12:25

With Dominic comfortably seated in his first-class seat, the sound of the plane's engines faded into the background, drowned out by the thoughts swirling in his mind. He should be focused on the high-stakes business meeting awaiting him in Paris, yet he could only think about Danielle. It unnerved him. Dominic was proud of his control, of his capacity to compartmentalise his emotions. Still, here he was, unable to keep Danielle out of his thoughts.

Isabella. Her name flickered in his mind, a memory that used to feel ever-present but was now fading. The realisation left him conflicted. He had loved Isabella deeply, and her loss had left an aching void. But now, Danielle's presence was filling spaces he thought would remain empty forever. Was this betrayal? Or was it a sign that he was prepared to move forward?

Dominic rested his head by the window, the city below shrinking as the plane ascended. He told himself that this trip would help him sort out his feelings, that distance would offer clarity. But in his heart, he knew the truth. Regardless of how far he travelled, Danielle had already made a home in his thoughts, and it was inescapable now.

Even though he didn't see Danielle every day, he was always aware of her movements, thanks to Andre's updates. It was a habit he hadn't questioned until now. Why did he feel the need to keep tabs on her? Did office gossip drive the concern for her well-being, or was there another reason? He sighed, conscious that he was only fooling himself if he tried to deny that his interest in Danielle went beyond mere professionalism. But admitting that was another matter entirely.

Danielle woke up that morning with a profound feeling of heaviness, both in her heart and spirit. The weight of everything she had been carrying, the relentless office gossip, her confusing affections toward Dominic and the long, exhausting days bore down upon her. She hadn't felt this drained for ages and the fact that she had skipped her usual 5 a.m. prayer session only heightened her awareness of the disconnection.

As she lay in bed, staring at the ceiling, Danielle felt a creeping sense of distance from God, a feeling she rarely experienced, but that always unnerved her when it came. She knew prayer was exactly what she required to combat this sensation, but the exhaustion running through her made it hard to muster the energy. Her efforts to connect with God felt increasingly futile, like she was stuck in quicksand.

Deep down, Danielle recognised this for what it was: a spiritual attack, a ploy to drive a wedge between her and God. The awareness of it did little to ease the emptiness she felt, though. The last few weeks had been a whirlwind of emotions and stress, leaving her feeling isolated and vulnerable, even in her moments of prayer.

Danielle knew she couldn't stay in this state for long. She needed reinforcement, the strength that comes from praying with her fellow believers. Her first thought was to call Ten, her closest friend and spiritual sister, who would understand and, more importantly, pray with her, help her navigate this storm and remind her of her strength that could only be found in God.

The scripture from 1 Corinthians 10:13 dropped in her mind, a faint beacon of hope amidst her struggle: *"No temptation has overtaken you except what is common to mankind. And God is faithful; he will not let you be tempted beyond what you can bear. But when you are tempted, he will also provide a way out so that you can endure it."*

Holding fast to that promise, she called Ten, feeling relieved when her friend answered after the second ring. Without preamble, she said "Do you have a few minutes to spare this morning?"

"Sure, usual spot?" responded Ten.

Danielle felt lighter as she sat across from Ten at their favourite café. The warm morning sunbeams filtered through the windows. Ten's broad smile and mischievous eyes were already working their magic, lifting Danielle's spirits.

"So," Ten began, leaning forward with a playful grin. "Does this have to do with a certain someone who is drop-dead gorgeous?"

Danielle rolled her eyes and laughed. "I knew you'd bring him up."

"Of course! Spill, Dani. I'm all ears."

Danielle recounted everything, the office tension, her dinner with Dominic, and the emotional turmoil that had followed. Ten listened intently, her earlier playful demeanour giving way to thoughtful concern.

When Danielle finished, Ten leaned back, studying her friend. "Is he a believer in God?"

The question caught Danielle off guard. She frowned, realising that in all the time she had spent thinking about Dominic, she had never once considered his faith. "I have no idea," she acknowledged.

Ten nodded thoughtfully. "Well, perhaps you need to find this out first before making any further decisions. This will be extremely crucial in determining your next steps. We know one thing for certain: he's not born again if the stories in the tabloids are to be believed! That might not be an issue if this is God's plan for your life. He will make a way for Dominic to give himself to Christ. I know this is unusual for you. Since Carter, you've never shown an interest in anyone else, so it's got to be quite conflicting."

Danielle sighed, realising the truth in Ten's words. "I just feel so conflicted. I didn't ask for these feelings and I refuse to let them lead me away from what I know is right."

"That's why you pray," Ten said firmly. "And ask the Holy Spirit to lead you. If Dominic's meant to be in your life, God will make it clear. But for now, guard your heart, Dani. Let God handle the rest."

Danielle nodded, taking in Ten's words. She had always admired her friend's wisdom and ability to cut straight to the heart of the matter. "Thanks, Ten. You always know what to say."

"That's what covenant sisters are for." Ten replied, her smile warm and reassuring. "Let's say a quick prayer."

The two friends joined hands, bowing their heads in prayer. Ten's voice was was steady and filled with warmth. "Lord, we come before you today, asking for your grace and wisdom. You see, Danielle's heart, her struggles, and her hopes. Help her trust in Your plan and to walk with courage and clarity. Guide her steps, Lord, and guard her heart against anything that isn't from You. Fill her with Your peace that surpasses all understanding and remind her she doesn't face any of this alone. Amen."

Chapter 16

There is nothing concealed that will not be disclosed, or hidden that will not be made known.

-Luke 12:2 NIV

Danielle arrived at work at around 10:00 a.m. and had just settled at her desk as her phone rang. It was Emily on the other side.

"Good morning, Danielle. Just a heads-up. Barbara's on the warpath, and unfortunately, you're her target."

The warning came swiftly, cutting through the usual morning pleasantries. Danielle paused, processing the words, but she wasn't entirely surprised. Still, hearing it spoken aloud confirmed what she had already suspected. Barbara wasn't just difficult. She was intentional.

"Me?" Danielle chuckled nervously. "What did I do?"

"I'm not sure, but she's definitely upset with you."

"Thanks, Emily, I appreciate the warning." She thanked God for Emily. She was definitely an ally.

As soon as Danielle hung up the phone, a sharp knock sounded on her office door. Before she could even respond, Barbara barged in without so much as a greeting. "Who do you think you are?"

Danielle was so taken aback that she couldn't muster a reply. Barbara took her silence as permission to unleash her fury.

Barbara narrowed her eyes, accusingly stating, "Dinner with Dominic doesn't grant you permission to arrive late without notice."

Danielle's mind raced. How on earth did she know about the dinner? The shock must have been visible on her face, because Barbara sneered and continued.

"Oh, you thought you were being discreet? I do not know what game you're playing, but I'm onto you. Pretending to be some virtuous woman when you're just a floozy!"

Finally snapping out of her paralysis, Danielle found her voice. "That's enough, Barbara. No one talks to me like that. I don't need to inform you of my every move. If you have concerns about my time, take it up with Human Resources. I won't tolerate this tone, and if you speak to me this way again, I'll file a formal complaint."

Danielle's voice was firm. "So, unless you have something constructive or work-related to discuss, I suggest you leave my office."

"You just watch!" Barbara spat, her face twisted with malice before storming out. Rage simmered beneath her exterior. She learned of the dinner from a friend who worked as a hostess at The Rubix. Knowing how she felt about Dominic, her friend had immediately informed her of the booking. Barbara seethed. She resolved she would make Danielle's life difficult and drive her out.

Danielle inhaled deeply to steady her racing heart. The morning's prayer session with Ten had lifted her spirits, grounding her in peace. But Barbara's venomous outburst had jolted her right back into the harsh reality of office politics. It was a stark reminder that faith and resilience would be just as crucial as strategy in navigating Pascale & Pascale.

Barbara's accusations replayed in her head, sharp and cutting. How had she even known about the dinner? Dominic had taken every precaution to keep it discreet, but it seemed privacy was a rare commodity in this office. That idea caused a chill down her spine.

"Why would Barbara have such an issue with me?" Danielle wondered aloud. She had always been professional, focused on her work, and careful to steer clear of office politics. Yet, despite her best efforts, Barbara had made her a target. She had to understand her enemy better if she was going to navigate this minefield successfully.

The answer, though frustrating, was clear. Barbara saw her as a threat and whether it was because of Dominic's attention or otherwise.

What she knew was that the situation with Dominic Pascale was becoming increasingly complicated. The attraction between them was undeniable, but she had always kept her boundaries clear, her professionalism intact. And yet, others were misinterpreting her intentions. Now, she was paying the price for something she never sought or encouraged.

She understood she had to handle this situation carefully. Barbara was clearly a formidable opponent, and Danielle needed to be strategic. Should she inform Human Resources or even Dominic himself? But she also preferred not to escalate the situation unless absolutely necessary. Reporting Barbara could backfire, and she was reluctant to give anyone the impression that she couldn't handle herself.

For now, she documented the encounter. Her chest felt tight, the lingering adrenaline making it hard to concentrate. The rhythmic clicking of her keyboard broke the silence in her office as she typed out a detailed account of Barbara's intrusion. Her fingers moved quickly, her pulse racing with each sentence she wrote. She could nearly hear Barbara's venomous tone again, the words echoing in her memory. Danielle paused, her eyes scanning the screen as she reread her account.

Her coffee sat forgotten beside her, now cold and stale. A faint sheen of sweat lingered on her palms, and she rubbed them absently against her skirt. With a deliberate click, she saved the email as a draft, her chest rising and falling as she exhaled slowly. The sharp tension in her shoulders eased slightly, but the weight of Barbara's threat still loomed like a dark cloud.

It was necessary for her to be on her guard. Barbara's threat, "You watch!" was filled with contempt. She also recognised that she needed to protect herself professionally and emotionally. Above all, she wanted to avoid becoming embroiled in office gossip or, worse, seen as someone who was using her assumed connection with Dominic to advance her career. That was not who she was, and she would allow no one to paint her in that light.

The week had flown by quickly and Dominic had just concluded an intense round of negotiations in France. They had made significant progress, but some details still needed tying up. He knew he would need to return and this time, he'd bring along an analyst who could speak fluent French. He made a mental note to have his PA check the company roster for anyone who met the criteria.

After the meeting, Monsieur Laroque Noir, the CEO, invited Dominic to Club Noir, an exclusive gentlemen's club he owned. Dominic recognised the unspoken implications. Declining wasn't an option, not if he wanted to maintain a strong business relationship.

Stepping inside, he took in the club's ambiance, tasteful, opulent, and distinctly masculine. The dim lighting, rich mahogany furnishings, and quiet hum of conversation created an atmosphere of refined exclusivity. Everything about the space exuded power and discretion, a sanctuary for men who thrived in the world of high-stakes business.

Upon arrival, a host ushered into a private room; then, two beautiful women appeared. One of them, stunning and confident, went straight to Dominic, settling onto his lap. Ordinarily, Dominic might have indulged in such an encounter, but as she smiled up at him, he felt no desire.

His mind betrayed him, comparing her overly made-up face to the natural beauty of Danielle's. Damn, there she was again, intruding on his thoughts without warning. With a polite but firm refusal, Dominic declined the woman's advances. She pouted, clearly disappointed, and left the room.

Monsieur Laroque chuckled, his eyes glinting with amusement. "Ah, Dominic, why send her away? She is... how do you say? Top shelf."

Dominic forced a polite smile, swirling his whiskey. "No offense, but I'm not in the mood."

"Not in the mood?" Laroque leaned back, his grin widening. "Or is there another woman occupying your thoughts?" His laugh was hearty, teasing, but it struck closer to the truth than Dominic cared to admit.

Dominic raised his glass, the cool weight of the crystal pressing into his palm as he swirled the amber liquid inside. The faint clink of ice against the glass punctuated Monsieur Laroque's teasing words. He brought it to his lips, the smoky warmth of the whiskey sliding down his throat, yet doing little to quash the mental turmoil consuming him..

The low hum of conversation in the private room receded as an image of Danielle rose unbidden. He could see her clear as day, her composed yet piercing gaze, the faint flush on her cheeks when she laughed, the way her voice carried an undertone of calm resolve. It was maddening how vivid she seemed, even in this dimly lit room, surrounded by opulence and distractions.

The scent of expensive cologne and cigar smoke was pervasive, but all Dominic could focus on was the faint memory of Danielle's delicate floral perfume, with a hint of something he couldn't quite place. He leaned back in his chair; the leather creaking softly beneath him as he tried to push her image from his mind.

"Ha, you've got it bad, mon ami," Monsieur Laroque retorted with a grin, clearly enjoying the situation.

Dominic stayed for another hour, engaging in polite conversation but never fully present. His thoughts kept drifting back to Danielle, and when the time finally came, he excused himself to prepare for his early morning flight back home. As he left the club, he felt a sense of relief. He was looking forward to going home, but more than that, he realised he was looking forward to seeing Danielle.

The week passed in a blur for Danielle. She kept her head down, immersing herself in work, determined to avoid any unnecessary interactions that might give Barbara more fuel for her scheming.

The whispers floating through the office were impossible to ignore, but Danielle refused to engage. She knew exactly where they originated. Barbara's handiwork was all over them.

Still, Danielle remained steadfast. She wouldn't defend herself against gossip. Her professionalism and work ethic would speak louder than any rumour.

By Thursday evening, she had completed the complex report she had been working on and handed it over to her manager. It was a relief to have it off her plate, and she was proud of the work she had done. Now, she could finally look forward to the weekend, a much-needed escape from the strain at the office.

Danielle had been eagerly anticipating this weekend. A spa retreat along with her mum, Ten, and Naomi were exactly what she needed to recharge. The thought of spending time with the women she loved most in a serene environment soothed her soul.

Warm saunas, soothing massages, and the laughter with her friends and mother filled her imagination. She packed her bags and a new book she had been saving for this trip. She couldn't wait to unwind and forget about the recent weeks.

As Danielle approached the group, her mother drew her into her arms. "There's my girl," Rose said cheerfully. "You look like you need this day as much as I do."

Ten, seated nearby and flipping through the spa menu, grinned. "She definitely does. I mean, if I had her job, I'd need a week in this place."

"Tell me about it," Naomi chimed in, her eyes shining with excitement. "But can we take a moment to talk about these treatments? I've booked the deep tissue massage because my shoulders feel like they've been carrying an immense load."

Danielle chuckled as she sank into the plush chair beside Naomi. "Honestly, that's how I've been feeling lately, too. A massage sounds like a dream. Let's get changed."

Ten minutes later, the four women settled into the spa's relaxation lounge, wrapped in soft robes with cups of herbal tea in hand.

"So, Danielle," Naomi began, her tone playful, "how's life at Pascale & Pascale? And, more importantly, what's the latest on Mr Tall, Dark and Brooding?"

Ten laughed, nearly spilling her tea. "Oh yes, spill the tea. I've seen his pictures in the tabloids, but you get to work with him up close. Is he really as scandalous as they say?"

Danielle sighed, a reluctant smile tugging at her lips. "He's not what I expected. The tabloids make him out to be this cold, untouchable billionaire, but that's not the man I see."

Her mum tilted her head, intrigued. "Then who do you see?"

Danielle paused, her tea swirling slowly in her cup. "Someone thoughtful. Reserved. He's been through real things that most people wouldn't understand. He's human, Mum. Flawed, like the rest of us."

Ten leaned forward. "So, what's the catch? There's always a catch with men like him."

"Well," Danielle admitted, "he's not perfect. He's still figuring out a lot like where he stands in life, what he really believes in. But I think that makes him real. Not some polished persona."

Her mum shot her a knowing look. "And how do you feel about all this, Danielle?"

Danielle hesitated, her cheeks flushing slightly. "I'm uncertain as of now. I'm trying to focus on work, but I can't deny there's something about him that makes me curious. Makes me want to understand him more."

Naomi nudged her playfully, a teasing glint in her eyes. "Sounds like someone's smitten."

Danielle rolled her eyes, but the warmth creeping up her neck betrayed her. "Hardly," she muttered, but Naomi wasn't convinced.

"You're incorrigible. It's not like that. He's complicated, and so am I."

Naomi raised a brow, her expression amused. "Complicated or interesting?"

Danielle sighed, knowing Naomi wouldn't let this go. "Both," she admitted reluctantly. "But right now, I'm here for one thing and one thing only. Relaxation, baby! Chocolate wrap or seaweed wrap?"

Naomi winked, "Chocolate, naturally," then the talk turned lighter, work momentarily forgotten, for a joyful experience.

A contented sigh escaped Danielle's lips as she sank into the warm embrace of the mineral-rich hot springs. The water lapped gently against her skin, its soothing heat seeping into her muscles, unwinding knots of tension she hadn't even realised were there. A faint herbal scent floated through the air, mingling with the soft melodies of a harp playing somewhere in the background.

She tilted her head back, allowing the steam to rise around her, a warm mist softly caressing her cheeks. The water shimmered under the dim overhead lights, casting a soothing dance of reflections across the surface.

With her eyes closed, Danielle focused on the sensations—the gentle ripple of water against her skin, the calming scent of lavender weaving through the air, and the faint hum of muffled laughter drifting in from the lounge. For a moment, the world outside faded, leaving only tranquillity in its place.

The next few days were a blissful escape. The conversations and laughter truly filled her heart. They shared stories, shared updates on their lives, and talked about everything from work, faith, to future dreams.

Chapter 17

The purposes of a person's heart are deep waters, but one who has insight draws them out.

-Proverbs 20:5 (NIV)

Dominic stepped off the plane, the hum of distant conversations and the rhythmic clatter of suitcases filling the background. He rubbed his temple, trying to shake off the weight of exhaustion and the lingering image of Danielle that had followed him across time zones. As he navigated the busy terminal, his phone buzzed in his pocket, the vibration startling him from his thoughts.

"Hey, D."

"Hey Dom. What's up? How was the meeting?" Daze's voice was upbeat as always.

"Meeting went reasonably well," Dominic replied, a hint of fatigue in his tone. "There are some loose ends that need tying up, though, so I'll have to make another trip soon."

"Ah, the joys of international business," chuckled Daze. "Well, you're back now. Let's catch up and don't think I've forgotten I'm due an update on Ms T."

Dominic sighed, knowing exactly where this was heading. Daze had been teasing him ever since he first mentioned Danielle, even though Dominic had barely scratched the surface of his feelings. But Daze, perceptive as ever, had picked up on something from their brief conversations.

"There's not much to tell, D," Dominic tried to deflect, but Daze wasn't buying it.

"Come on, Dom. I've known you too long. You don't get distracted by anyone, but this woman has you tied up in knots."

Dominic walked toward the exit, the automatic doors sliding open to the cool morning air. He hesitated before responding, not knowing how to put his thoughts into words.

"It's complicated," he finally said. "She's different and I can't get her out of my head and it's messing with me. There's an innocence about her man. I have a feeling she's a virgin!"

Daze emitted a low whistle. "Bro, that's deep. If she's untouched, that's rare, man. You don't find women like that every day. She's definitely a keeper."

Dominic sighed again, leaning against a pillar as he waited for his driver. "I don't know, man. I'm hesitant to mess things up for her. She's got a good thing going, and I'd rather not be the reason she gets hurt."

"That's why you must be clear with yourself first," Daze advised. "You can't go into this half-heartedly. If you think there's something there, follow up on it with honesty. Otherwise, leave her alone."

"Yeah, you're right," Dominic admitted. "I'll figure it out. I just need some time."

"Well, whatever you decide, I'm here for you," Daze said. "But I'm warning you now, if you break that girl's heart, I'll kick your ass."

Dominic chuckled, feeling unexpectedly lighter after the conversation. "Noted, D. Noted." A smirk lingered in his voice. "We'll catch up properly at Mum's tomorrow."

"Sounds good. See you then," Daze replied before hanging up.

As Dominic slid into the back seat of his chauffeured car, he stared out the window, his thoughts once again drifting to Danielle. Daze was right. Maybe it was time to find out what he really wanted.

The day after, Dominic and Daze visited Mrs Pascale for their usual Sunday dinner, a tradition that had become a comforting routine. As they walked into the house, Carla, or "Mum" as both men called her, greeted them with open arms.

"How are my babies doing?" she said, cuddling them both tightly. Carla considered Daze her son as much as Dominic; Daze had also had long since realised that motherhood transcends blood ties. He was eternally grateful for the unwavering love and support he had received from both Carla and Dominic over the years. It had shaped him into the man he was.

"Hi, Mum," they both replied in unison.

"Who you calling babies? Can't you see the titans you're speaking to?" Daze joked, flexing his muscles dramatically.

Carla chuckled, "Make yourselves comfortable, boys. I'm just finishing up dinner."

"Mum, why do you insist on cooking dinner yourself when you have staff who can do this?" Dominic asked, puzzled as always by her insistence on preparing the meal.

"You'll never get it, Dom. I enjoy doing this. It keeps me grounded, helps me remember where I came from," she replied with a smile, brushing off his concerns.

With that, they poured drinks of neat whiskey on the rocks and made their way outside to enjoy the evening air on the patio. Dinner, when it was served, was a feast of perfectly roasted potatoes, fresh vegetables, and succulent chicken, the rich aromas wafting through the air. Carla, ever the gracious hostess, ladled gravy on the plates as her sons exchanged playful banter.

"Mum, you spoil us with these meals."

Carla waved him off with a laugh, her hands brushing against the starched white apron tied around her waist. "And don't you forget it."

The three of them sat around the table, catching up on life, as was customary. As the conversation flowed, Carla couldn't resist her usual probing. "So, when are you two going to give me my grandkids?" she asked, her eyes twinkling with playful expectation.

"I think Dom will be the first," Daze replied, waggling his eyebrows mischievously. Dominic responded by kicking Daze under the table, making them all burst into laughter.

Carla was about to follow up with another question when the butler appeared at the patio entrance. "Madam, you have a guest," he announced politely.

The lighthearted atmosphere dimmed when the butler's announcement cut through the laughter. Vivienne strode onto the "Good even Mom, Dominic, Daze. It's a full house today," she said, her voice brimming with charm. "I thought I'd drop by to visit Mum, since it's been ages."

Daze stiffened, barely masking his distaste. He was not a fan of Vivienne, always considered her shallow and fake. Dominic simply lacked the desire to deal with her presence. Even Mrs Pascale, ever the gracious host, was annoyed that Vivienne interrupted her precious time with her sons.

Still, they all greeted Vivienne with forced smiles and she took a seat, apparently unaware of the tension she had brought with her. They served dessert shortly after, and the conversation became stilted and polite. Because of the change in mood, Daze was the first to leave. "Well, it's been great, but I've got to get going." He stood, kissed his mom, and said goodbye.

"I should get going too," Dominic added, rising from his seat almost immediately after Daze.

Dominic and Daze exchanged knowing looks, walking out of the house, both relieved to be away from the uncomfortable atmosphere. The night air was cool against Dominic's face as he stepped outside, the sound of their footsteps crunching on the gravel driveway breaking the quiet.

Daze gave a low whistle, shaking his head. "Man, she really knows how to kill a vibe," as they reached their cars.

Dominic chuckled, though his thoughts were already drifting. The distant sounds of the city served as a backdrop to his internal conflict.

"I know what you mean," Dominic agreed.

"Well, at least the food was good," Daze said, trying to lighten the mood.

"Yeah, mum always delivers," as they said their goodbyes.

Vivienne lingered after Dominic and Daze left, seizing the opportunity to spend uninterrupted time with Carla. She had been carefully orchestrating more visits lately, weaving herself deeper into the fabric of the Pascale family.

To Vivienne, it was all part of a larger strategy solidifying her status as the future Mrs Dominic Pascale. She knew that earning Carla's favour was the key to securing her position, and she played the part perfectly: attentive, charming and ever so supportive.

But tonight had rattled her. Dominic's behaviour, his abrupt departure with Daze, a glaring reminder of the growing gap between them. Vivienne tried to brush it off, blaming Daze as she always did, but deep down, a gnawing fear took hold. Dominic's coldness wasn't something she'd accounted for and it threw her carefully laid plans into uncertainty.

Still, she put on a warm smile, engaging Carla in light conversation. If Dominic was slipping away, she was resolute in tightening her grip, starting with his mother's unwavering approval.

As they occupied the comfortable, tastefully decorated living room, Vivienne probed. "So, how's Dominic doing, mum?" she inquired, her tone relaxed but her eyes sharp, trying to read any unspoken hints in Carla's response.

Carla smiled warmly. "Oh, he's good. Why don't you ask him yourself?"

Vivienne hesitated. "Well, he's been very distant lately," she admitted, and hoped Carla would open up. Carla's expression didn't change, but she gave a slight nod, as if Vivienne's observation did not surprise her.

"Do you think he's now open to moving on after Isabella?" Vivienne asked, her voice carefully neutral, though the question carried significance.

Carla looked at Vivienne thoughtfully. "Dominic has been through a lot since Isabella," she said slowly, choosing her words with care. "But moving on is something he'll have to decide for himself. It's not something anyone can rush."

Vivienne carefully hid her disappointment behind a tight-lipped smile. She'd hoped for a clearer answer, some sign that Dominic might finally be willing to let go. But Carla's response, though gracious, offered no such reassurance. "Of course," Vivienne said smiling. "I just want what's best for him, you know?"

Carla returned the smile with equal politeness but added a gentle edge to her replied. "I'm sure you do, dear. But Dominic's choices are his own."

The subtle firmness in Carla's words stung. It wasn't unkind, but it served as a reminder that no matter Vivienne's intentions, she had no claim over Dominic's future.

Vivienne's heels clacked sharply against the polished floors as she made her way to the door. Outside, the cool evening air brushed against her skin. The streetlights cast elongated shadows across her sleek car, their cold glow matching the steely resolve that had had solidified in her chest.

Behind the wheel, she gripped the steering wheel tightly; her knuckles whitening as her mind raced. The conversation with Carla had left her disheartened, but not defeated. She turned the key, the engine purring to life.

Her car turned onto the winding driveway of her home, the gates creaking open as she punched in the code. Having pulled to a stop,

Vivienne sat silently for a moment, staring at her reflection. Her jaw tightened, her eyes hardening with determination. "This isn't over."

Chapter 18

May integrity and uprightness protect me, because my hope, Lord, is in you.

-Psalms 25:21

Danielle entered the office on Monday morning, feeling a renewed sense of purpose. The butter-yellow peplum dress she had chosen radiated optimism. Her white pumps clicked confidently on the gleaming floor as she walked. The soothing memories of the spa retreat lingered, bolstering her resolve to tackle whatever challenges the week would bring.

Danielle was looking forward to the 9:30 a.m. Initiative Meeting. It was a rare opportunity for employees to present ideas aimed at enhancing the company's initiatives. A space where innovation met purpose.

She had meticulously refined her pitch; her focus on an internship program designed to empower young women from diverse ethnic backgrounds. This wasn't just another corporate initiative to her, it was personal.

Danielle understood firsthand the barriers to success, the silent obstacles that came with being an outsider in elite spaces. She believed in the transformative power of opportunity, and this program had the potential to open doors for others just as she had fought to open them for herself.

The room buzzed with chatter as the senior team settled in. Danielle walked in, her nerves tempered by determination. She surveyed the room, noticing Barbara seated near the centre, her gaze hard and cold. Danielle didn't let it faze her. This was too important.

As the meeting progressed, Danielle's turn finally arrived. She felt a fleeting wave of nerves, but quickly steadied herself. She stood confidently, holding her notes but barely glancing at them.

"Good morning, everyone," Danielle began, her voice steady and assured. "My proposal is an internship program designed to provide under represented minority women with valuable work experience and mentorship. Many women, like myself, have faced significant obstacles growing up. I believe this program can help break down those barriers and give talented young women a fair shot at success."

As her words settled over the room, a thoughtful silence followed. Danielle sensed that some of her colleagues were moved, their expressions showing both interest and quiet agreement. But from her peripheral vision, she caught Barbara smirking. It was subtle, but unmistakable. A silent challenge. Danielle held her ground. She hadn't come this far to be intimidated, least of all by Barbara.

"We need to invest in the next generation; this begins with creating spaces where we can nurture diverse voices."

Barbara's derisive laugh pierced the room. "Planning to flood this place with more of your kind?" her question creating a vacuum like effect within the room. Danielle's grip on the conference table tightened.

"My kind?" her voice was tranquil but edged with steel. She let her gaze lock onto Barbara's, her expression unwavering. "If by that you mean talented, hard-working individuals who deserve a chance, then yes, Barbara. That is exactly what I'm proposing. And it's not flooding, it's investing. Something this organisation could benefit from."

Barbara's sneer faltered. She hadn't expected Danielle's push back. A palpable tension was present, like the stillness before a storm. A faint shuffling of papers and the shifting of chairs filled the silence as senior members exchanged uneasy glances.

"This initiative is about creating equal opportunities. It's about offering a chance to those who rarely get one. I'd think a company with Pascale & Pascale's reputation would value that kind of progress. If we truly want to reflect the communities we serve, we must actively invest in their future. I believe this internship program will not only help these young women but also enrich our company."

A few people politely clapped, though Barbara's offensive remark muted and clouded the room's energy. The meeting moved on, but the tension lingered. As the session wrapped up, Danielle collected her things, refusing to make eye contact with Barbara again.

This wasn't about handouts or optics. It was about equity, progress, and the undeniable advantage of inclusion. But Danielle wouldn't waver. She had spoken her truth, and she wasn't backing down.

Not long after the Initiative Meeting concluded, Danielle's inbox pinged with a new email. Only a subject line.

Subject: Meeting Room. 10 Minutes

She stared at the screen, a flicker of unease settling in. No context. No details. Just a cryptic summons. With a steady breath, she straightened her posture, grabbed her notepad, and prepared herself for whatever awaited.

Anxiety, anticipation, and tension washed over Danielle as she entered the room. The atmosphere was thick with unease and she could sense that something significant was about to unfold. The mood in the meeting room felt colder when Dominic walked in later that morning, his presence immediately commanding attention. His sharp, deliberate steps echoed in the silent room. Without preamble, he spoke to the group.

"We are here to discuss a comment made during the Initiative Meeting." The faint click of a pen in someone's hand was the only sound as he spoke the offensive remark aloud. 'Planning to flood this place with more of your kind?" Danielle's stomach tightened, but alongside the nerves, she found validation. Someone had reported Barbara's comment and now it was being addressed at the highest level.

Barbara, sitting a short distance from Danielle, stiffened, her face betraying a flicker of unease. She fidgeted in her seat, then cleared her throat, her voice defensive but laced with forced calm. "I was only joking, Mr Pascale," she said, her words edged with defiance, her gaze darting toward Danielle with thinly veiled hostility.

"Joking?" Dominic's sharp retort cut through her excuse like a whip. "How dare you dismiss such an offensive remark as a jest? Or have you conveniently forgotten that I, too, am her kind?"

His words hit hard, leaving no room for rebuttal. Barbara's face flushed, but she remained silent, her usual bravado extinguished. Danielle kept her composure, though her heart raced, feeling both vindicated and unnerved by the sudden confrontation.

Everyone held their breath as he continued angrily. "This will go on your formal record, Barbara. Racism, in any form, is absolutely unacceptable in my company, especially not from senior management."

Barbara's face flushed crimson, her usual confidence faltering under Dominic's piercing gaze. The room felt heavier, the silence stretching just long enough to unsettle her.
She stammered, "Sorry, Mr Pascale. It won't happen again."

Her voice lacked its usual sharpness, the forced apology a clear sign she understood Dominic wasn't someone to test. Dominic's eyes narrowed, his expression turning steely. His voice, cold and clipped, cut through the air with unmistakable authority.

"Why are you apologising to me, Barbara?" The question wasn't just rhetorical, it was a challenge. A warning. His tone left no room for misinterpretation, the weight of his words pressing down like a silent verdict.

Barbara's gaze flickered toward Danielle, her lips tightening, before she forced out a clipped, "My apologies, Danielle. That was inappropriate of me. It won't happen again."

Danielle inclined her head slightly. The apology felt hollow, more a box-ticking exercise than a genuine acknowledgment of wrongdoing.

Dominic didn't let up. His gaze swept across the room, his tone blistering as he addressed the group. "And the rest of you? Your silence is complicity. Every single one of you had a responsibility to speak up, and you failed. Consider this your warning. I expect integrity and courage from my team. This will not happen again."

When he finally dismissed the group, the pressure snapped like a tightened wire breaking free. Chairs scraped against the floor as people hurried out, their faces pale and drawn, eager to escape the suffocating atmosphere.

No one wanted to linger. No one wanted to be the next target of Dominic Pascale's scrutiny. Danielle stood to leave.

"Ms Thompson, a word, please."

Dominic's hard exterior softened as he stepped toward Danielle, his usual rigid posture easing slightly. His voice, though steady, carried a rare sincerity.

"Danielle, I'm sorry you had to endure that. No one should."

Danielle met his gaze, the initial wariness in her eyes melting into quiet gratitude. There was no doubt, he had taken this seriously.

"Thank you, Dominic," she said, her voice measured but genuine. "I appreciate that."

Dominic nodded, his expression earnest. "I heard you handled yourself well in there. I'm impressed."

Dominic's eyes held hers. "If anything like this happens again, come to me. Directly."

"I will. Thank you."

Chapter 19

Your desire grows inside you until it results in sin. Then the sin grows bigger and bigger and finally ends in death.

-James 1:15

Friday arrived in a flash. Danielle peered at her desk clock, 3:50 p.m., when the sound of a knock at her door broke her concentration. "Please come in," she invited, and Emily entered with a familiar grin.

"Second time's the charm. We're all heading to the bar after work. Want to join?"

Danielle offered an appreciative smile. "Thanks, Emily, but I won't be able to make it." She hesitated briefly before she added, "I'm not being ungrateful, Emily. I'm a born-again Christian. I don't drink or go to pubs or bars. It's just a personal conviction."

Emily's expression softened with understanding. "I get it, and appreciate you sharing that. Some people were curious, but honestly, I really like you, Danielle. I know there's been talk lately, but I don't buy into the rumours."

Danielle felt a warm surge of gratitude. "Thank you, Emily. That means a lot. Maybe we can grab coffee instead sometime? I'd also love to invite you to my church."

Emily chuckled. "The coffee sounds good, for sure. Church? Maybe. I'll mull it over."

After Emily left, Danielle decided she could afford to leave work a little early. She had plans to meet her friend Ten and her husband, Terrence, at a chic restaurant in central London. They were celebrating Ten's new collaboration with a well-known clothing brand, and Danielle had heard that the steaks there were among the best.

Later that evening, Danielle arrived at the restaurant where she was meeting Ten and Terrence. The space exuded warmth and sophistication, the soft glow of lights reflecting off polished wood and brass accents, creating an inviting environment.

She scanned the room and quickly spotted Terrence, already seated. A smile broke across her face as she approached, greeting him with their usual hug and a friendly kiss on the cheek.

"Right on time," he teased, his eyes twinkling with familiarity.

"Of course," she replied smoothly, sliding into her seat. "I wouldn't want to keep you waiting."

"Ten's running late," Terrence explained with a grin. "But don't worry, I've got plenty of jokes to keep you entertained."

Danielle laughed, instantly at ease as Terrence launched into one of his witty stories. They chatted easily while waiting, the hum of conversation and the occasional clink of glasses forming a pleasant backdrop.

Across the restaurant, Dominic sat with Vivienne, who was mid-sentence about an upcoming gala, her voice carrying the effortless charm she always employed in his presence. But his attention drifted the moment Danielle walked in.

It wasn't intentional, it was instinctive. Dominic's gaze tracked Danielle as she moved through the room, her effortless poise drawing him in without effort. The soft flicker of a smile graced her lips as she approached a table where a lone man sat waiting. Meanwhile, Vivienne continued speaking, unaware that Dominic's focus was no longer on her.

Her casual yet effortlessly elegant ensemble highlighting her toned figure and a carefree confidence. She was breathtaking. His chest tightened as she laughed with the man sat at her table. Jealousy flickered unexpectedly, startling him. Who was he? What was their relationship? And why did it bother him so much?

A few minutes after arriving, Danielle excused herself to the ladies' room. Dominic, whose eyes had never strayed from her since the moment she walked in, made a split-second decision.

Without hesitation, he pushed his chair back and muttered a curt, "Be right back," to Vivienne, barely registering her reaction.

His focus was elsewhere. Tracking Danielle.

"Dom?" Vivienne's confusion went unanswered as he quickly strode off.

Danielle emerged from the restroom when a firm yet gentle hand guided her into a dimly lit alcove. She opened her mouth to protest, but froze when she met Dominic's intense gaze.

"Dominic?" she asked, with confusion and disbelief. "What are you doing?"

"Who is he, the guy you're with... who is he to you?"

Danielle stared at him, incredulous. "Mr Pascale, do you even hear yourself? What does it matter to you? You're my boss, not my friend, and certainly not anything more. My private life is none of your business!"

Her words challenged him. Dominic's expression faltered, and he let out a frustrated breath. "Sorry, I am surprised to see you here, especially since I've been thinking about you, and it's been driving me mad. I know this might be inappropriate, but tell me I'm not the only one feeling... this."

Danielle's breath hitched as his words sank in. The heat of his hand brushed hers, sending a jolt of electricity up her arm. She pulled her hand back, crossing her arms defensively. "Dominic, this isn't appropriate. I—"

"I got it wrong," he said, his voice filled with self-reproach. "Let's just forget this happened. Enjoy your evening." He started turning away.

"No, Dominic, wait, I was just... I feel it too, but my Christian values and the fact that you're my boss complicate things."

Before she could finish, approaching footsteps broke the moment. Without thinking, Dominic stepped closer, pulling her deeper into the shadows. Their proximity was intoxicating. Danielle's heart pounded as she felt his warmth, his presence overwhelming her senses. Danielle's heart was racing and Dominic could barely keep his composure.

The temptation to close the small gap between them, to lean in and kiss her, was overwhelming and he could tell from the pounding of her heart and the change in her breathing that she was thinking the same. Dominic leaned down, his lips brushing her forehead in a lingering kiss that sent a shiver down her spine. "We'll talk about this another time. For now, I'll leave you to your evening."

Danielle nodded, unable to find her voice, her heart hammering as if it might leap from her chest. The sensation of his kiss lingered on her skin, a quiet moment of tenderness that left her breathless and more conflicted than ever.

Dominic retreated, his hand brushing hers briefly before he turned and disappeared down the hallway, leaving her standing there in the dim light of the alcove. She pressed a shaking hand to her brow, closing her eyes as she tried to gather her thoughts.

What was she doing? This wasn't her. She had always prided herself on her self-control, her firm adherence to her principles. And yet, Dominic Pascale had unravelled her resolve with a single moment.

As she walked away, she couldn't escape the memory of his touch, his words, or the look in his eyes. The line between right and wrong felt impossibly blurred, and in an unprecedented moment, Danielle felt utterly lost.

Returning to her table, Danielle fought to regain her composure. Her hand trembled as she smoothed her hair, the lingering sensation of Dominic's kiss etched into her skin. Terrence noticed her flushed face immediately.

"You okay, Dani? You look flustered," he remarked, his brow furrowing.

"I'm fine," she replied quickly, forcing a smile. "It's quite warm in here."

Meanwhile, Dominic returned to Vivienne's table, masking the turmoil inside him. "Is everything alright?" she asked, her tone tinged with suspicion.

"Yes, something needed my attention."

Back at Danielle's table, Ten finally arrived, her energy filling the space as she hurried toward them.

"Sorry I'm late, guys! Traffic was a nightmare," she said breathlessly, wrapping Danielle in a warm hug before turning to her husband, pressing a lingering kiss to his lips.

From a distance, Dominic watched the exchange, and relief washed over him. So, the man wasn't Danielle's date. The unexpected tension in his chest eased, but that he'd felt it at all left him unsettled. Why had it mattered so much?

"No worries, Ten. We were just catching up," Danielle replied, grateful for the distraction.

The rest of the evening passed in a blur for both Danielle and Dominic, each lost in their own thoughts, unable to shake the charged moment they had shared.

Danielle struggled to fully engage in the warmth and laughter of her friends. She smiled, nodded at the right moments, but her mind kept drifting back to the alcove, the intensity in Dominic's eyes, the tension crackling between them, the unspoken weight of his presence.

Meanwhile, Dominic found himself equally distracted. No matter how hard he tried, he couldn't ignore the way she had unravelled his usual control with nothing more than her presence. The memory of her refusing to be dismissed.

They had parted ways, but something had shifted. And they both knew it.

That night, as Danielle lay in bed, the dim light from her bedside lamp cast soft shadows on the ceiling. She relived the encounter with Dominic in an endless loop, her thoughts loud. Her hand brushed the cool fabric of her pillow as she shifted, trying to get comfortable.

He was magnetic, yes, but it wasn't solely his charisma that drew her in. A fragility was present in him that tugged at her heart and despite her best intentions, she couldn't deny she felt irresistibly drawn to Dominic.

This wasn't just an ordinary attraction. It felt deeper, more consuming, and infinitely more dangerous, and it bothered her. How had she, someone so rooted in her convictions and morals, allowed herself to be swept up in this?

As the weekend unfolded, the pair found themselves ensnared in a whirlwind of emotions. For Dominic, the memories of the alcove and Danielle's confession clashed with the ghost of Isabella's memory. He sat in his apartment, guilt and longing battled within him. Isabella had been his anchor and the idea of moving on from her felt like disloyalty.

But Danielle had ignited a spark he hadn't felt in a while, and it was both exhilarating and terrifying. Unable to process these emotions alone, Dominic called Daze, his only confidant who always offered solace without judgment.

Over steaming cups of coffee in a quiet café, Dominic poured out his heart. "Daze, I feel like I'm forgetting Isabella," he admitted, his tone thick with guilt. "I never thought I'd feel such affection for anyone else. It feels like I'm betraying her memory."

"Dom, you loved Isabella, and she loved you. But she's gone. Moving forward doesn't mean forgetting her. It means honouring the life she wanted for you. A full life filled with love and happiness. Some people never get a second shot at love. You have. If Isabella were here, do you think she'd want you to cling to guilt, or to embrace what's in front of you?"

Dominic nodded, absorbing Daze's words. Letting go of the guilt wasn't easy, but for the first time, a glimmer of hope surfaced, maybe he could explore what he felt for Danielle without dishonouring Isabella's memory.

Meanwhile, Danielle wrestled with her own inner turmoil. As she sipped tea in her living room, it did little to soothe her racing thoughts. At 27, Danielle knew her choice to remain a virgin wasn't exactly trendy. In a world where people often bragged about early sexual experiences, she recognised that her decision might invite curiosity or even ridicule.

For her, this wasn't about conformity; it was a deeply personal commitment. She learned from a young age that her body was God's temple, a vessel to be honoured. Sex wasn't just physical; it was the ultimate sacred act binding not only bodies but souls. A spiritual exchange, a mingling of spirits, and until she was with someone who understood and cherished that vision, she'd rather wait than compromise on something so profound.

Danielle reached out to Ten and, as was their custom, met for coffee, where Danielle poured out her heart, once again confessing her burgeoning feelings for Dominic and the guilt that came with them.

"Ten, I don't have a clue what to do," Danielle said, her hands clasped tightly around her mug. "It feels as though I've crossed a line, like I've betrayed everything I stand for. This connection with Dominic goes against my values. I know better."

"Dani, you're human. We all feel things we don't expect, it's part of life. What matters now is clarity. You need to figure out where Dominic stands in terms of his beliefs and values. Does he share your faith? If not, this will only get harder."

As Sunday evening settled over the city, Dominic and Danielle found themselves at a crossroads, their thoughts consumed by the uncertainty ahead.

For Dominic, it was about reconciling his past with the possibility of a future with Danielle. For Danielle, it was about facing a connection that tested her deepest convictions.

They couldn't avoid each other forever. The intensity between them demanded resolution. But for now, they sought clarity, hoping that in time, the answers they needed would reveal themselves.

Chapter 20

Teach me to do your will, for you are my God! Let your good Spirit lead me on level ground!

-Psalms 143:10

Monday morning arrived far too quickly for Danielle. Her alarm buzzed insistently, pulling her from a restless sleep. She began her day as she always did, kneeling in prayer, her hands pressed together, whispering words of surrender and seeking guidance. Journaling followed, the scratch of pen against paper grounding her thoughts. But even as she closed her notebook, a lingering sense of anxiety refused to fade.

"Danielle," she muttered aloud, pacing in her bedroom. "It's not a big deal. You might not even see or speak to Dominic today. Pull yourself together. Remember, you're not doing this alone, the Holy Spirit is there to guide you. Do not rely on your own intellect."

Determined to channel that confidence, she chose her outfit with care: pleated wide-leg trousers in a striking cobalt blue, paired with a white-and-blue blouse that exuded professionalism. The sleek heels added an extra touch of poise.

At 6:45am, Danielle reached her office and the sight of a bunch of white daisies on her desk stopped her in her tracks. Their fresh, dewy petals glowed under the soft office light. She leaned in, sniffing the sweet scent filling the air, a smile gracing her face. She searched for a card, but none was there. Curious, she went for her phone to text Ten, but paused when she received a message.

"Like the flowers?"

Her smile widened as she typed back quickly.

"Yes, thank you. A nice surprise."

"Just nice?"

"Delightful surprise?"

"You're a tough customer."

Danielle laughed, "Bye, Mr Pascale."

Danielle smiled as she put her phone down, her heart racing from the brief but playful exchange with Dominic. She attempted to concentrate, but the bouquet of daisies on her desk kept drawing her attention. The flowers were far beyond a thoughtful gesture. They were a message, one that made her heart flutter with both excitement and anxiety.

As the morning passed, Danielle peeked at her phone more often than usual, half-expecting another message from Dominic. But as the hours ticked by, silence followed. A part of her was relieved, as she needed time to sort through her feelings without the added pressure of interacting with him.

Just before lunch, she heard a rapping. It was Emily, holding a folder. "Hey, Danielle. Just dropping off the revised project. Beautiful flowers," she remarked with a playful smile.

"Thanks, Emily," Danielle said, trying to keep her tone casual. "They were a surprise."

Emily was clearly curious, but not wanting to pry. "Well, whoever sent them has good taste. Please, inform me if you need anything else."

By the time lunch rolled around, Danielle decided she needed a break. She grabbed her phone and headed outside for a walk, hoping the fresh air would clear her mind. As she strolled through a nearby park, she reflected on her conversation with Ten over the weekend. She realised she needed to have a serious conversation with Dominic about his beliefs.

She was about to return to her office when her phone pinged.

"How's your day going?"

"It's been busy. Just taking a break to clear my head."

"Good idea. Want to grab a coffee later?"

Danielle smiled. She wanted to say yes, but realised that she must set some boundaries before things went any further.

"Not today, perhaps end of the week?"

"Ok. I'll keep you to it."

By midday Wednesday, the office buzzed with anticipation. Danielle had spent hours perfecting her presentation for the pivotal board meeting, meticulously analysing data and refining her recommendations.

Her tailored navy dress fit flawlessly, exuding confidence and authority, while a delicate pendant rested at her collarbone, a subtle yet personal touch.

She was ready! When the meeting started, the polished mahogany table stretched before her, lined with sharp-eyed board members who listened intently. Dominic was among them, sitting a short distance away, his gaze heavy on her.

Her voice rang clear as she delved into her report, detailing how her strategies had directly influenced the bank's recent surge in profits. She gestured smoothly, her tone a blend of professionalism and passion. The room was was silent, save for the rhythmic click of pens and the soft rustle of papers.

When she finished, there was a beat of silence before the room erupted into applause.

"Exceptional work, Ms Thompson," one board member said, leaning forward with an approving nod.

"This kind of foresight is exactly what we need." Another chimed in, "Your analysis has been spot-on. The results speak for themselves."

She thanked them graciously, her voice steady, despite her heart racing with exhilaration. This was what she had strived for, a moment of validation for her effort and expertise. As the meeting concluded, the board members filtered out, murmuring praise.

Danielle collected her notes with deliberate calm, but her senses prickled as she felt Dominic's approach. His cologne, subtle and woodsy, reached her before he spoke.

"Impressive presentation," his voice was low enough that only she could hear. His tone was neutral, but his eyes conveyed pride and admiration.

"Thank you, Mr Pascale. I'll speak to you later." The energy between them was simmering, but she couldn't afford to let her emotions slip now, not before her colleagues.

The moment Danielle stepped out of the boardroom, her resolve was put to the test.

"Well done, Danielle. You certainly know how to put on a show," Barbara remarked, her tone dripping with thinly veiled sarcasm.

The snide comment barely registered in the face of her achievement. She had proven herself today, and no one, not even Barbara, could diminish that.

Danielle didn't break stride, a cool smile gracing her lips. "Thank you, Barbara. I aim to deliver."

Just as Danielle boarded the elevator, her phone buzzed. Seeing Carter's name light up on the screen brought an instant smile to her face.

"Hey, Dani. I'm in your area for a bit. How about we catch up over lunch? It's been too long."

"Carter! I'd love that. Meet me in 20 minutes?"

Her heart lifted at the thought of seeing him. After such a high-pressure day, reconnecting with him felt lucky. At the front desk, Carter stood waiting, tall and composed, his warm smile instantly setting her at ease. His presence felt like stepping into a time capsule. A reminder of a simpler, more predictable time in her life.

"Danielle, you look amazing," Carter exclaimed, his voice genuine as his eyes swept over her. "I'm glad to see you."

"You too, Carter. It's been a while," she replied, returning his hug with equal warmth.

As they exited the building, their conversation flowed effortlessly, filled with laughter and shared memories. Danielle felt a mix of nostalgia and reassurance. While their lives had diverged, the connection they shared remained intact.

Danielle and Carter settled at their private table at Lazzo Lez. The quiet murmur of conversation from other diners blended with the gentle clinking of cutlery, creating a cosy atmosphere and the aroma of freshly baked bread and rich Italian dishes wafted through the air.

Carter leaned back slightly, a relaxed smile on his face as he glanced over the menu. "This place is amazing," he remarked, his eyes lighting up. "You've really upgraded your taste since our university days. Remember when we thought a pizza deal with unlimited soda was the peak of luxury?"

Danielle laughed, her eyes sparkling at the memory. "How could I forget? We practically lived at that pizzeria. And to think we called that dining out."

Their banter flowed effortlessly, light-hearted and familiar, as if no time had passed. When the server arrived to take their orders, Carter smirked, deferring to her recommendation of the lobster ravioli.

"Let's hope you've outgrown overcooking pasta," he teased, his eyes glinting with amusement.

Danielle rolled her eyes, but the warmth in her smile gave her away. Some things never changed.

"So," Carter began, leaning forward, his tone curious, "What's been happening in your life? Work, love, the total package?"

Danielle hesitated, swirling her glass of water as she considered her response. "Work's been good, challenging, but rewarding. I've been working on some extensive projects which have kept me busy."

"Sounds like you're thriving," his voice was warm with admiration. "You always had a knack for balancing a million things at once. It's good to see you so in your element."

"And you?" Danielle asked, "A great job, a fiancée. What's she like?"

Carter's face softened. "Amelia's incredible. She's smart, funny and keeps me grounded. I think you'd really like her. She reminds me of you actually, kind, driven and no-nonsense."

Danielle's heart warmed. "She sounds wonderful, Carter. I'm so happy for you."

"Thanks, Dani," he said, using the nickname he'd always called her by. "It feels good, you know? But enough about me. What about you? Are you seeing someone special?"

Danielle hesitated, her gaze flickering down to the glass of water in her hands. "Not exactly," she said finally. "The situation is complicated right now."

Carter tilted his head, concern flashing across his face. "Complicated how? Are we talking bad first date complicated or life-altering drama complicated?"

Danielle laughed, but it didn't quite reach her eyes. "Somewhere in between, I guess. Let's just say I'm figuring things out."

Carter studied her for a short while, appearing pensive. "Well, if anyone can figure it out, it's you. Just remember, you deserve someone who sees how amazing you are."

Danielle's heart warmed at his words. "Thanks, Carter. You've always known how to lift my spirits."

"That's what friends are for," he winked. "Speaking of which, we need to agree not to let so much time pass before our next lunch. Deal?"

"Deal."

Their conversation turned reflective, dipping into memories of their shared past. Carter's tone grew serious as he said, "Dani, I've been meaning to tell you I owe you so much. Back then, I thought we could make it work no matter what, but you saw the truth before I did. You saved us both from a life that wouldn't have been right for either of us."

His words surprised her. "Carter, you don't have to. "

He held up a hand, gently cutting her off. "No, let me say this. You would have been so unhappy being a housewife, Dani. Witnessing the sparkle in your eyes while you talk about your job, your projects, your life, now that you are in that position, is exactly where you should be. That's a joy I don't think I could have ever given you."

Touched by his words, Danielle felt a tightness in her throat. She smiled warmly, her heart full of gratitude for his understanding. "Carter, that means a lot. I'm glad you found happiness too. We had some good times, didn't we? But you're right, it's all worked out for the best."

He nodded, his expression reflective. "Yeah, we did. And look at us now, both happy and thriving in our ways. I think that's the best outcome we could've hoped for."

Danielle reached across the table, briefly squeezing his hand. "I couldn't agree more. Here's to new beginnings and enduring friendships."

"To new beginnings," he echoed, raising his glass in a toast, their laughter mingling with the hum of the restaurant, a testament to the enduring bond of a friendship that had stood the test of time.

Carter had just leaned over to kiss Danielle on the cheek in a gesture of warmth and gratitude when Dominic entered the private section of Lazzo Lez. His sharp gaze zeroed in on the scene, and his chest tightened. Danielle's free smile and affectionate eyes stirred unprepared emotions in him. She wouldn't have coffee with him, but there she was, laughing and sharing an intimate moment with another man. A surge of jealousy rose before he could tamp it down. Dominic approached their table, his footsteps deliberate, his expression carefully neutral.

Danielle spotted him first, her eyes widening slightly. "Mr Pascale," she greeted, her tone measured. "What a surprise."

"Not Dominic?" he replied smoothly, his manner casual, but his gaze filled with condemnation.

Danielle flushed slightly, her composure faltering. "Oh, where are my manners?" she said quickly, recovering. "Dominic, this is Carter, an old friend from university. Carter, this is Dominic, my boss."

Carter extended a hand, his smile friendly. "Nice to meet you, Dominic."

Dominic shook his hand, his grip firm, almost pointed. "Likewise."

"Well," Dominic said after a pause, his eyes briefly flickering between them, "I'll let you two enjoy your lunch. Danielle, I'll see you at the office later."

Danielle's chest tightened with an emotion she couldn't quite name. Carter, ever observant, didn't miss a beat.

"Dani," he said softly, "that's the complication you mentioned earlier, isn't it?"

She sighed, not trusting herself to speak. Carter pressed gently. "Is he saved?"

"No."

"Does he believe in God?"

"I haven't a clue," she said, frustration seeping into her voice.

Carter's expression turned serious. "Dani, don't go into this blindly. Have you prayed about it?"

"Yes!"

"Then pray some more," Carter said gently but firmly. "Don't save yourself from me only to find yourself in a worse situation."

Danielle's euphoria from earlier had evaporated, replaced by heaviness. Carter's words had pierced through her, leaving her with questions she wasn't quite ready to confront. Ten, now Carter, both emphasising the same points. As they approached the foyer of her workplace, a solemnity weighed on both of them had replaced the earlier ease of their reunion.

Carter stopped and faced her. "Dani, I hold you dear and want you to be happy. But remember, shared faith and values should form the foundation of any relationship, especially one as complicated as this. Without that, you're setting yourself up for heartbreak."

Danielle averted her gaze, her thoughts a tangled web of emotions. She felt an undeniable connection to Dominic, something she hadn't experienced in years, but Carter's words rang painfully true. Her faith had always been her guiding compass, and the thought of compromising it filled her with dread.

"I know you're right. It's just difficult. There's something there, Carter, and I can't ignore, but I know I can't let it cloud my judgment either."

Carter's hand rested gently on her shoulder, his touch warm and grounding. "Dani, pray about it. Really pray. And listen. Don't rush into anything before you're sure it aligns with who you are and what you believe."

Danielle nodded, grateful for his wisdom and concern. "Thank you, Carter. I mean it. I appreciate you looking out for me."

"Always." "Take care of yourself, okay?"

He drew her into a brief hug, and she held on a moment longer than normal. A mix of gratitude and uncertainty filled her heart. She offered a hushed prayer for clarity and strength as he left. The daisies on her desk from earlier that week were a distant memory, their warmth replaced by the cold reality of the decisions she now faced.

The week went by quickly, Dominic's absence conspicuous. No messages, no calls. Just silence. By Friday evening, around 7:00 p.m., Danielle stood in her office, looking out at the city skyline as the setting sun bathed the buildings in hues of gold and orange. The sound of her office door creaking open interrupted the quiet. Without turning, she knew instantly who it was, and she'd been half-expecting this moment, though his boldness or stupidness, dependent on one's view, to visit her office at this time, still took her by surprise.

Dominic stood in the doorway, hesitating for a moment. His face shadowed, his expression unreadable. He attempted to convince himself to stay away, to let things cool down. But the picture of Danielle with Carter on Wednesday, laughing, sharing a moment he wasn't part of, had unravelled his resolve.

"Danielle, I know I shouldn't be here, and I have no intention of making things more complicated. But I couldn't leave things as they were after Wednesday."

He stepped further inside the room, closing the door gently behind him, the soft click amplifying the tension hanging in the air. As he stood beside her, a light brush of their arms sent a jolt through them both.

Danielle didn't move, her gaze fixed on the view. "Dominic, I think we both know this is crossing a line."

He exhaled, his breath warm and unsteady, ignoring her comment and countered it with a question. "You feel it too, don't you? This pull between us, I'm not imagining it, am I?"

Her heartbeat sped up at his words, but she forced herself to stay composed. She turned slightly, meeting his gaze. His eyes searched hers, brimming with another layer of vulnerability she hadn't seen previously.

"We'll talk," Danielle said firmly, though her tone softened as she presented him with a small smile. "But not here, not like this."

Dominic's shoulders relaxed slightly, relief flickering across his face. "Whenever you're ready," he murmured.

For a moment, neither moved. His fingers brushed against hers, his touch eliciting the usual effect. Their hands lingered, neither willing to pull away first.

Danielle's cheeks warmed, but she broke the silence with a soft, "Goodnight, Dominic." her voice gentle, resolute, a quiet reminder that boundaries still mattered.

"Goodnight, Danielle." His hand reluctantly shifted away. He turned and left, the sound of the door clicking shut behind him echoing in the office's stillness.

As the door closed, Danielle let out a shaky breath, her hand instinctively pressing against her chest. The warmth of his touch lingered, as did the unshakable awareness that this was far from over. She crossed the room to her desk, sitting down heavily as her thoughts swirled.

The view outside her window had shifted from the golden hues of sunset to the deep blue of twilight. The city lights twinkled like stars, a stark contrast to the storm brewing inside her. She whispered a prayer for strength to navigate the path ahead without losing herself.

Dominic, meanwhile, walked through the quiet halls to the elevator, his footsteps echoing in the silence. His mind was a whirlwind of emotions—relief, confusion, and an elusive feeling he couldn't quite name. As he stepped into the elevator, he leaned against it, closing his eyes, letting out a long, measured breath.

They both knew that the conversation they'd deferred would change everything. The only question was whether they were ready for what lay ahead.

Chapter 21

Wine is a mocker, strong drink a riotous brawler; And whoever is intoxicated by it is not wise.

-Proverbs 20:1

After leaving Danielle's office on Friday, guilt clawed at him relentlessly. The memory of Isabella haunted him, her laughter echoing alongside the steady voice of Danielle. Every thought of Danielle, a step away from a love he had sworn to cherish forever. In his desperation to silence the noise in his head, Dominic picked up the phone and called Daze.

"What's up, Dom?" Daze's voice carried its usual warmth, laced with curiosity.

"Let's go out, Daze. I have to forget for a while."

Daze chuckled, clearly surprised. "Finally taking a night off? Meet me at Sobo Lounge in thirty."

The crowded club was loud, just as Dominic had hoped. The pulsing beat drowned out his thoughts and for the first time in a long while, he surrendered to the chaos. Daze, always up for a party, kept the drinks coming, laughing and joking with Dominic as they found a booth secluded from the noise.

After a couple of rounds, Daze leaned in, eyeing Dominic carefully. "So, are you finally ready to address it?"

Dominic sighed, swirling his drink. "Address what?"

"About why you called me up tonight and spare me the I just wanted a night out nonsense."

Dominic chuckled, albeit weakly. "You know me too well. It's everything. Danielle, moving on, Isabella's memory, the guilt. It's tangled up and messing with my head. You must think by now I'm a broken record."

"Look, Dom, better to be a broken record, than a pressure cooker waiting to blow. I've got you. You mustn't torture yourself for feeling something new. It's natural you're alive, after all. Loving Isabella doesn't mean you can't be open to whatever might come next."

"It just feels wrong, Daze. The idea of being with someone else, it feels like I'm leaving her behind, forgetting, erasing her memory."

Daze placed a hand on his shoulder, giving it a firm squeeze. "It's living, not erasing, and you have every right to that and you know Isabella would want that for you."

"How do you know that?" Dominic asked, almost desperately. "It's easy to say from the outside."

Daze paused, then leaned forward, meeting Dominic's gaze with a seriousness that brooked no argument. "I know it because it's true, man. I've seen people get trapped by grief and guilt, like you're doing. They end up carrying around so much weight that they can't move forward, can't love anyone, not even themselves. I used to be there, Dom. You know that better than anyone."

Dominic looked away, feeling both the validity of Daze's words and the sting that came with them. How could he forget what his brother went through? "Sorry, D, that question was callous. I have no idea what's right anymore."

"That you're questioning it proves how deeply you cared for her. But life isn't about staying frozen in one moment, Dom. It's about honouring the past, yes, but letting it guide you instead of trap you." He smiled softly, "You're a good man. Let yourself believe you deserve a second chance at happiness."

He had a sip of his drink, grinning softly to break the tension. "Plus, man, Danielle's a catch. You're not exactly throwing your life away here."

Dominic smirked. "So now you're my therapist?"

"More like your conscience," Daze shot back with a wink. "Now come on, loosen up. Tonight's your night off, remember?"

The two shared a laugh and Dominic felt lighter. The conversation was like a lifeline, reminding him he wasn't alone in his struggle and that maybe he could feel alive again.

As the night wore on, Dominic's composure slipped further, the drinks hitting harder than he intended. His laughs grew louder, his steps less steady, and soon he was leaning heavily on Daze, who had been watching him closely all evening. Daze, realising his brother had reached his limit, steadily guided Dominic through the crowded club to the exit.

Dominic, barely coherent and mumbling half-formed thoughts about Isabella and everything he couldn't let go of, leaned into Daze when they got to the car. When they pulled up to Dominic's home, he was nearly asleep and Daze practically carried him in, ensuring he got to bed safely.

The week slipped by in a blur of activity for both Dominic and Danielle, each absorbed in their respective worlds. Dominic buried himself in work, using the busyness of the week as a shield against the guilt and confusion that had plagued him over the weekend.

He avoided any unnecessary communication, especially with Danielle, fearing that speaking with her might stir up the emotions he was desperately trying to suppress.

The week brought little reprieve for Danielle. She noticed Dominic's absence at a scheduled meeting, but didn't dwell on it. Instead, she leaned on her faith, pouring her emotions into prayer and worship. Gospel music filled her apartment in the evenings, each song reminding her to trust God's plan and not rush into decisions that could compromise her values.

When Friday afternoon arrived, Danielle was finishing her reports when Emily appeared, her excitement infectious.

"Have you found your dress for the fundraising gala?" Emily asked with a grin.

Danielle smiled, shaking her head. "Not yet. But I'll start looking soon. I'm excited about it."

The annual charity fundraiser was one of the most anticipated events on the company's calendar. Each year, Pascale & Pascale hosted this grand affair, bringing together employees, business partners, and key stakeholders to raise funds for selected charities.

This year, the spotlight was on mental health initiatives, a cause that had drawn significant attention and generous donations. Excitement buzzed through the office, as the event promised not just philanthropy, but a night of networking, prestige, and influence.

Danielle was genuinely excited about the gala. It wasn't merely a night of glitz and glamour; it was also a prime networking opportunity. She was bringing Ten, Naomi and her mum as her guests. Ten's clothing brand was gaining traction, and Danielle knew the gala could open up new opportunities for her friend to network and expand her business.

As she returned home that evening, Danielle reflected on the silence between her and Dominic. Perhaps this was God's response to her prayers and the distance might be a blessing in disguise. She focused on the gala and the joy it would bring, tucking her feelings for Dominic deep into the recesses of her mind.

Unknown to Danielle, Dominic watched from the shadows as she departed the office that evening. Did she feel nothing from his silence, or was she simply better at hiding her feelings? The realisation that he might not matter as much to her as she did to him only deepened his turmoil.

At home, Dominic gravitated toward the piano. The instrument, once a source of solace, now betrayed him. The melodies he played felt hollow, the notes disjointed. Frustrated, he slammed his hands against the keys, the discordant sound reverberating through the space.

In a fit of rage, he tossed a vase to the other side of the room, watching as it shattered into fragments, a reflection of his own fragmented emotions.

Still seething, he stormed to his gym, channelling his anger into a punishing workout. Sweat dripped from his brow, his muscles burning as he pushed himself past his limits. Despite his efforts, Danielle remained firm in his thoughts.

By the weekend, Dominic, along with Danielle, was steeling themselves for the imminent charity gala. For Danielle, it was an opportunity to immerse herself in a cause she cared deeply about while supporting her friends.

For Dominic, it was a chance to refocus, to remind himself of his role as a leader and philanthropist. But inwardly, both carried unspoken questions and unresolved feelings. The gala loomed as more than just an event. It was a stage for potential confrontation, resolutions, or unexpected reactions.

Chapter 22

He who loves transgression loves strife and is quarrelsome; He who [proudly]
raises his gate seeks destruction [because of his arrogant pride].

-Proverbs 17:19

That weekend, Vivienne's brunch took an unexpected turn. Sat
on the sunlit patio of an upscale café, sipping her mimosa with
practiced elegance, laughing lightly at her friend's quip when a polite
but nervous voice interrupted.

"Good morning, Ms Fox," the woman began, clutching her
handbag like it was a lifeline. "You may not remember me, but I work
at Pascale & Pascale. Dominic is my boss."

Vivienne's initial instinct was irritation. She rarely entertained
interruptions during her private moments, but Dominic's name
immediately piqued her interest. Her poised smile masked the flicker
of curiosity behind her gaze.

"Oh?" she said smoothly, setting down her glass. "And by what
means are you acquainted with me?"

"I've seen you and Dominic open the fundraising ball with the
first dance every year. You two look so perfect together," the woman
offered, her voice brimming with admiration.

Vivienne's smile widened. Her vanity stroked. "That's very kind
of you. What's your name?"

"Barbara," she replied, with a display of feigned humility.

"I hope Dominic is treating you well?" Vivienne inquired, her
voice light but laced with calculated intent.

Barbara hesitated, lowering her gaze before responding, "Oh,
absolutely. He's a great boss, but..." she let the word linger in the air,

her tone conspiratorial. "Sometimes, I worry people take advantage of his kindness."

Vivienne arched an eyebrow, intrigued. In Vivienne's experience, people rarely paired Dominic and kindness in the same sentence. "Dominic, kind? That's hard to imagine."

Barbara lowered her voice. "Well, he's been acting out of character lately and there's a lot of talk about him spending time on the 14th floor, visiting a top financial analyst named Danielle."

The name struck Vivienne like a bolt of lightning. Dominic previously mentioned it; however, she didn't investigate further, as planned. Now, the pieces were falling into place and she didn't like the picture they painted.

"I appreciate you sharing, Barbara. It's been a pleasure meeting you. Keep in touch," and she handed Barbara a sleek business card, masking her simmering emotions behind a veneer of politeness.

As Barbara walked away, satisfaction flickered across her face. She had planted the seed. Vivienne, meanwhile, stirred her drink thoughtfully. So, this Danielle, could she be the reason for Dominic's distraction? The gala will be the perfect opportunity to remind him of who truly belongs by his side.

For Danielle, Dominic's fortnight of quiet had been a blessing in disguise. At first, she had questioned it, wondering if she had pushed him away, but as the days passed, she found herself grateful. The stillness had enabled her to refocus on her priorities. Through prayer, work, and church services, she felt stronger and more at peace than she had in weeks.

The charity gala was all anyone could talk about at work and the night had finally arrived. Whispers about the high-profile guest list and speculations on Vivienne and Dominic's iconic opening dance were everywhere.

Danielle paid little attention. While the event was undeniably glamorous, she was more excited about celebrating with her mum and friends, who would join her for the evening.

Her dress for the gala, a flowing emerald green gown, was a perfect reflection of her style, understated yet elegant. As she checked her appearance before leaving, she couldn't help but smile. Tonight wasn't about anyone else; it was about showing up as her best self.

Before heading out, Danielle checked her phone one last time. No messages from Dominic. She no longer felt the absence, and she resolved to ignore him at the gala.

Chapter 23

Let not yours be the outward adorning with braiding of hair, decoration of gold and wearing of fine clothing, but let it be the hidden person of the heart with the imperishable jewel of a gentle and quiet spirit, which in God's sight is very precious.

-1 Peter 3:3-4

Vivienne had spent a fortnight meticulously planning for the gala, knowing it was her best opportunity to reclaim Dominic's attention. Despite their long history, his recent aloofness worried her.

Barbara's reassurances that Dominic hadn't interacted further with Danielle afforded her a brief sense of control, but it wasn't enough to suppress her doubts. This gala wasn't just an event. It was her stage. Her chance to remind Dominic exactly where he belonged.

Tonight, she wouldn't leave anything to chance. Attired in a striking red gown that clung to her figure, Vivienne embodied confidence and allure. The off-shoulder design and thigh-high slit commanded attention, while the cascading waves of her hair and flawless makeup completed the look.

Vivienne knew she looked stunning, and tonight, she planned to remind Dominic of the role she was meant to play in his life. As her car arrived at the hotel, Vivienne took a deep breath, her carefully constructed poise masking the storm of determination within. *Tonight will be unforgettable.*

Dominic stood before the mirror, his reflection staring back at him. The custom-made black suit fit perfectly, but his sharp appearance did little to calm the turbulence inside. For two weeks, he had kept his distance from Danielle, enforcing a self-imposed silence, he told himself, was necessary. But it was both penance and purgatory, each day amplifying the tension between his emotions and his guilt.

Dominic knew he couldn't avoid her tonight. The mere thought of seeing her filled him with equal parts dread and longing. Would she be cold and indifferent or warm? His jaw clenched as he adjusted his tie. He knew one thing: his restraint would face a test, no matter what happened tonight.

He cast a swift glance at his watch. The moment arrived to meet Daze and his mum in the foyer. Dominic considered how ironic it was that amidst a high-profile gala meant for charity and celebration, he was preparing for what felt like a personal confrontation. He sighed, adjusting his suit jacket. Only time would tell how this night would unfold.

At 7:00 p.m., the entrance of the hotel was a spectacle of elegance and sophistication. The red carpet stretched out before the hotel doors, guiding a sea of well-dressed guests into the lavish event. Celebrities, politicians, business tycoons and employees alike mingled, each more glamorous than the next.

Photographers lined the carpet, capturing moments as people arrived in sleek cars, escorted by valets. The guests moved with a sense of confidence, their designer dresses and tailored suits sparkling under the brilliant lights.

The air crackled with excitement and anticipation. Conversations flowed and laughter resonated through the space as attendees greeted each other, exchanged pleasantries and posed for photos. The Grand Hotel, known for hosting only the most prestigious events, was aglow with warm golden lights, enhancing the glamour of the night. Every detail from the flower arrangements to the champagne flutes, carried by attentive servers, was immaculate.

The ceilings inside the grand ballroom were high, adorned with intricately detailed chandeliers, casting a warm radiance throughout the space, walls covered in rich velvet drapes and large, arched windows that let in the soft light of nightfall. The floor was a polished marble that reflected the glow of the chandeliers, adding to the magnificence of the room.

At the far end, a grand staircase swept down from a balcony, designed for the dramatic entrance of guests. Polished stone formed the stairs, and a rich dark wood banister, ornately carved with gold accents, supported them. Each step was wide and shallow, putting guests at ease as they descended into the ballroom. At the base of the staircase, elegant floral arrangements and candelabras added to the grandeur, welcoming guests as they arrived.

Fine linen-covered round tables, each topped with crystal centrepieces and golden cutlery, filled the ballroom; musicians in a corner softly played classical music, filling the room with its sound. An aura of timeless elegance and luxury pervaded the space, making every entrance feel like a moment from a fairy tale.

Dominic, always a stickler for time, arrived first. As he made his way through the grand ballroom with his mother and Daze, his charm and natural confidence were on full display, effortlessly greeting guests and engaging in small talk, but beneath the surface, his thoughts was on Danielle. He scanned the room, hoping for a glimpse of her amid the crowd.

Daze, always perceptive, noticed Dominic's wandering eyes. With a knowing grin, he nudged his brother. "Looking for someone?" he teased lightly.

"Whom?" Dominic replied, attempting to brush off the question with feigned innocence.

Daze couldn't hold back his laughter, clapping his brother on the shoulder. "Alright, bro, we'll play it your way. However, I know exactly who you're looking for."

Vivienne paused atop the staircase, the epitome of poise. Her striking red gown caught the light, drawing everyone's attention. She basked in the attention, her smile radiant as whispers of admiration rippled through the crowd. But her focus was singular: Dominic.

She expected him to approach as he always had, to escort her down with his usual charm. Instead, Dominic remained rooted in place, his expression polite but distant. The slight dimmed her smile, though she recovered quickly, descending gracefully while greeting onlookers. When she reached Dominic, Vivienne's composure had returned. "Dominic," she greeted with practiced warmth, placing a hand lightly on his arm.

"Vivienne," he replied, his tone cool but courteous.

Daze, watching the interaction, bit back a grin. "Ah, the wanna be Mrs Pascale has arrived," he teased, earning a quick glare from Dominic.

Danielle's arrival was unplanned elegance. A minor wardrobe mishap with Naomi had delayed their group, but it didn't matter. As they reached the top of the stairs, their laughter and camaraderie carried through the room like a breath of fresh air.

Danielle's emerald green dress was a vision of understated beauty. The intricate gold and silver embroidery caught the light, while the modest slit and soft V-neckline balanced confidence with grace. Her accessories, simple gold earrings and a delicate bracelet, perfectly complemented her ensemble. She moved effortlessly, exuding an unforced radiance that captivated everyone present.

Dominic's breath caught. Time seemed to slow as he watched her descend, her laughter a melody that resonated above the room's din. Her presence was magnetic, eclipsing everything else. She wasn't trying to command attention, but she had everyone's, including his. Daze produced a low whistle. "Damn, bro, she's something else."

Dominic took an involuntary step forward, drawn by an unseen force, only to feel hands on him.

Vivienne's grip was subtle yet firm, a silent claim wrapped in poise and possession. She didn't need to speak; her touch said enough.

Daze placed a steadying hand on his brother's shoulder, a grounding force amid the quiet storm brewing within him. "Not now. Play it smart."

Vivienne followed his gaze, her confidence unravelling as she realised the depth of his focus. Danielle wasn't just another woman, she was *the* woman. Another one who appeared to be replacing Vivienne, again.

Dominic swore under his breath. He knew Daze was right. Walking over to Danielle during this high-profile event would only stir up unwanted attention and fuel rumours. The notion of other men watching her, their eyes lingering on her in that stunning dress, made his blood boil.

His hands balled into fists at his sides. He fought the primal urge to protect what he felt was his, but she wasn't. Not until he could figure out how to reach her again.

"Damn it!" He kept his gaze fixed on Danielle and he could see the attention she was drawing, the glances, the curiosity and while she laughed and carried on with her friends, seemingly unfazed, he couldn't shake the possessiveness that gripped him. If anyone dared cross a line with her tonight, Dominic knew his restraint would snap.

Chapter 24

A heart at peace gives life to the body but envy rots the bones.

-Proverbs 14:30

Danielle was aware of Dominic's gaze, its intensity unmistakable, like a current pulling her toward him despite the distance. She hadn't laid eyes on him; however, she knew he was there. That magnetic force between them, undeniable as ever, hummed faintly in the back of her mind. Focus, Danielle, she reminded herself. He's had two weeks to speak. He chose silence. Whether it was God's protection or Dominic's indecision, she wouldn't let it distract her now.

Danielle stood tall, her laughter genuine yet measured, effortlessly blending into the vibrant energy of her companions. She refused to let Dominic see the cracks his absence had left behind. Not tonight. Tonight, she was poised, present, and in control.

Across the ballroom, Dominic stood with Vivienne at his side, her hand casually looped around his arm. The image they presented was one the world expected of him. But he felt anything but composed. He was too aware of Danielle's presence.

Vivienne sensed his distraction. With a tighter clasp on his arm, and a smooth, calculated voice, she leaned in. "Dom," she her tone laced with quiet urgency. "You're missing your own party. Let's make the rounds."

Dominic let himself be led, knowing exactly what Vivienne was doing. Her desire was to be seen with him, to mark her territory in the most subtle and effective way. While they wove through the crowd, exchanging pleasantries with guests, Dominic's gaze kept straying. He spotted Danielle's table, with her turned from him, her laughter lighting up the space.

Finally, Dominic saw his opportunity. Heart thundering, he excused himself from the conversation, his steps purposeful as he approached Danielle's table.

Naomi noticed him first, her raised eyebrow and sly smile betraying her amusement.

Sensing the shift in energy, Danielle turned just as Dominic arrived.

"Good evening, ladies," Dominic greeted, his voice smooth and strong. "I hope you're enjoying the evening."

Naomi and Danielle's mum responded warmly, while Ten her knowing smile was full of unspoken commentary. "We certainly are," Ten said, her gaze flicking briefly to Vivienne, who stood just behind Dominic, her hand still resting on his arm. "It looks like you are, too."

Dominic fixed his eyes on Danielle's, searching for a sign, anything beyond polite indifference. "Danielle."

"Mr Pascale," she answered,evenly, the use of his formal title deliberate, a subtle barrier she erected between them.

The coolness of her response was a blow. Dominic faltered, unsure how to break through the wall she'd built. Beside him, Vivienne's smile faltered as she followed his gaze, noticing his focus on Danielle.

She flashed a dazzling smile at the group to assert herself. Seizing the moment, she chimed in, "It's been such a wonderful evening so far. Dominic always hosts the most exquisite events."

Ten, couldn't resist. "Yes, we've noticed," she remarked with a sweet but piercing smile.

Vivienne's smile tightened, though she maintained her outward composure. "One must live up to the expectations of such a grand event," she replied smoothly, her gaze shifting to Danielle. With feigned politeness, she asked, "I'm Vivienne. Are you a business associate of Dominic's?"

It was a calculated move, a subtle assertion of her position. Danielle, unflustered, met Vivienne's gaze. "I'm an employee and these are my guests," she replied firmly.

Then, with a serene smile, Danielle added, "And you're Mr Pascale's childhood friend, if I'm not mistaken?"

Lop Vivienne stiffened slightly, the jab hidden beneath Danielle's measured politeness not lost on her. "Indeed," she responded coolly. "Dominic and I have been close to each other for years."

"Childhood friendships are rare and valuable." Danielle retorted. Her words carried no malice, but the neutrality in her voice unsettled Vivienne further. *This Danielle is no pushover,* she thought.

Naomi glanced at Ten, raising an eyebrow as if to say, *is this really happening?* Ten, ever the provocateur, leaned in with a sweet smile. "It's always fascinating how people from the past find ways to stay relevant, isn't it?"

The comment had its intended effect and Vivienne visibly reacted; her smiled dropping sharply, her grip on Dominic's arm tightening. "Well," she stated, her tone frostier now, "it was nice meeting all of you. I'm sure we'll see each other throughout the evening."

Danielle smiled, "I'm sure we will." Although polite, her tone showed a quiet strength that was absolutely clear, she wasn't intimidated.

Vivienne turned to leave, but Dominic lingered for an instant longer. He wanted to say something to bridge the gap between him and Danielle. But her composed demeanour held him at bay.

"Enjoy the rest of your evening," Dominic said finally, his voice low, almost hesitant.

Danielle nodded her head, her serene expression unchanging. "You too, Mr Pascale."

Dominic left, his heart heavier than before. Danielle's calm defiance leaving him both impressed and frustrated. She was untouchable tonight, and it only made him want to reach her more.

Dominic and Vivienne, as was customary, proceeded to the centre of the floor at the announcement of the first dance. Vivienne beamed, her smile wide and triumphant, basking in the crowd's adoration. Danielle, like everyone else, was compelled to watch. Even she had to admit they looked striking together.

The orchestra began, their steps perfectly synchronised, a performance honed by years of practice. But for Dominic, the moment felt hollow, his movements mechanical. He barely registered the audience or Vivienne's radiant smile. Danielle occupied his thoughts with a force that made every step with Vivienne feel like treachery.

Danielle, seated with her family, maintained a stoic expression, but a heavy ache settled in her chest. She convinced herself it didn't matter; Dominic's life and choices were his own.

However, Dominic's presence with Vivienne evoked feelings she couldn't handle. The room grew stifling, the force of her emotions pressing down on her. Quietly, she rose and slipped onto the balcony, the gentle evening air offering a reprieve.

Dominic noticed the moment she left. Her departure sliced through the practiced choreography like a razor's edge and the second the music ended, he bowed to Vivienne, murmured a polite excuse and left her on the dance floor.

Vivienne struggled to maintain her composure as whispers swirled around her. She lifted her chin, forcing a smile that didn't reach her eyes, her heart sinking. Despite how much effort she had put into the evening, she knew Dominic's thoughts weren't with her.

Danielle stood in solitude on the balcony, the city lights glittering like distant stars against the skyline. The breeze brushed her skin, carrying the sound of the party behind her. She clutched the balcony railing, trying to steady herself. *Why does this bother me so much? She wondered. What right do I have to feel like this?*

The soft sound of footsteps behind her interrupted her thoughts. She didn't need to turn around to know whom it was.

"Danielle," he murmured, his voice subdued and uncertain.

She stiffened, willing her racing heart to calm. Slowly, she turned to face him, her expression guarded. "Mr Pascale," her voice, erecting the barrier she desperately needed.

"Don't do that," Dominic exclaimed, his frustration evident, his voice edged with something raw.

"Please."

The single word hung between them, heavier than the space that had grown in his self-imposed silence.

Danielle's eyes searched his face, looking for answers in his furrowed brow and the shadow of regret that lingered in his expression. "Why are you here, Dominic?" "Shouldn't you be inside with your *guests*?" Her emphasis on the last word was sharp, leaving no doubt about whom she meant.

Dominic stepped closer, not breaking eye contact. "I'm where I need to be."

Her frustration flared, emotions she had kept in check for weeks bubbling to the surface. "You're delusional," she snapped. "That's what you are! Have you forgotten this past fortnight, your silence? And now you show up here, as if nothing happened?"

Dominic's hand moved slightly, as if to touch her, but he hesitated, letting it fall back. "Danielle, I'm sorry. I never meant to hurt you."

She scoffed, stepping back. "No, you're not sorry. Do you think you can just come in and out whenever it suits you? You're arrogant, just like everyone says." Her words cut deep, though she knew there was more behind them than her conscious self would allow her to admit. "We have nothing in common, Dominic. I'm just an employee and that's all we'll ever be. Let's keep it that way."

A flash of dark emotion passed over Dominic's face. His jaw clenched, his eyes narrowing slightly, though his voice remained steady. "Danielle, you don't understand. This isn't about you."

"Right," she interrupted bitterly. "It's not me, it's you. How original." The moment she voiced her thoughts, guilt washed over her. *That wasn't fair*, she thought, feeling a pang of regret. *Oh, Danielle, get a hold of yourself. Don't let anger control you. This isn't Christlike, this isn't who you are.*

Danielle's pulse quickened, an unfamiliar sensation stirring within her. She'd never been one to lose her composure so easily, but clearly, her attraction to Dominic was unravelling her in ways she wasn't used to.

Her thoughts spiralled, torn between the potent attraction she felt and her principles that screamed the very essence of this conversation was wrong.

She drew a deep breath to steady herself. "I apologise." "That was out of line. But Dominic, I doubt this can happen. We come from different worlds and I'm unwilling to be part of whatever mess this is."

"My pastor always says if you wish to know the true essence of a man, see how he reacts in times of hardship," she continued, holding Dominic's gaze. "We haven't even given this," she gestured between them, "a name yet, and at the first sign of trouble, you're running."

Her voice softened, but her words landed with precision. "This says a lot about your emotional availability or perhaps, more accurately, your unavailability."

There was no malice, just the truth. A truth Dominic couldn't ignore.

Dominic looked down, gathering his thoughts, before meeting her gaze. He moved nearer, his voice steady but pleading. "You're right. I've been selfish and I've handled this poorly, but this isn't easy for me, Danielle. With you, it's different, and I'm unsure how to handle this."

Danielle crossed her arms over her chest as she made a step back, her resolve wavering. "What exactly do you want from me, Dominic?" she asked pointedly.

"I want you," Dominic said simply, the raw honesty making her heart stumble. "I lack knowledge of what the future looks like, and I don't have all the answers, but I know I can't walk away from this without trying. You make me feel alive as I haven't in a while. But I'm terrified I'm not capable of this, again."

The stillness between them was thick with unspoken emotion, a tension neither of them dared to break.

Danielle's breath hitched at his confession, her body reacting before her mind could catch up. Unbidden thoughts crept in, thoughts that were definitely not Christian-like.

For a fleeting moment, she saw past Dominic's confident exterior to the man beneath. Vulnerable. Uncertain.

But that vulnerability wasn't enough. It didn't erase the doubts that gnawed at her, nor did it silence the voice reminding her why she had been keeping her distance in the first place.

She turned away, her voice softer now. "Dominic, you're asking me to trust you, but grand gestures or intense words don't build trust. It's built on consistency, on actions and faith."

"I know, and I've failed you, and I intend to fix it, if you'll give me the chance."

Danielle looked at him, her heart conflicted between the connection she felt and the principles she'd always adhered to. "I need time," she declared at last.

Dominic nodded, his eyes reflecting a combination of understanding and longing. "Take all the time you need. I'll wait."

For a short time, they stood in silence, the cool night air wrapping around them like a fragile truce. Then, without another word, Danielle turned and walked back inside, leaving Dominic isolated on the balcony.

Chapter 25

For I can see that you are full of bitter jealousy and are held captive by sin.'

-Acts:8:23

Vivienne had been lurking nearby, bidding her chance. The moment Danielle disappeared from the balcony, she slipped in. Her presence shattered Dominic's solitude like a pebble tossed into a still pond. She slid her hand down his arm in what she intended to be an intimate gesture, but Dominic's entire body stiffened, his shoulders squaring with tension.

He didn't turn to face her. His eyes remained fixed on the skyline, his jaw tight. "What do you want, Vivienne?"

Despite the sharpness of his voice, she continued, speaking softly yet with calculated intention. "We've known each other for so long, Dom. I've been by your side through everything. Even when Isabella..."

At the mention of Isabella's name, Dominic spun around, his eyes blazing with fury. "What gives you the right to say her name?"

Vivienne flinched but refused to back down. The years of suppressed feelings and simmering bitterness burst to the surface, fuelling her determination. "Why?" she demanded, her voice rising. "What made her special that you chose her over me? What did she have that I didn't?"

Dominic's expression grew grimmer, his fists clenched by his sides as he struggled to rein in the torrent of emotions that threatened to overwhelm him.

"She's been dead for 18 months, Dominic!" Vivienne continued, her tone turning shrill. "Dead! And nothing you do can bring her back.

You walk around like she's still here, haunting you. And now you're moving on with Danielle! She's not even in your league. She's just a,"

"Vivienne." Dominic's voice was a low, menacing growl that stopped her mid-sentence. "You're treading on dangerous ground. Shut your mouth before you say something you can't take back."

But Vivienne was too far gone, her jealousy and pain blinding her to reason. "No, I will *not* shut up," she shot back fiercely. "You're going to listen to me, Dominic! I've loved you for years, stood by you through everything, watched you with all your women, and turned a blind eye. I know you better than anyone else! I'm the one who can stand by your side as your equal, as your partner—"

"You're sick in the head, Vivienne," Dominic spat, cutting her off. His tone was icy, each word laced with disdain. "Why would you settle for a life like that, begging for scraps? I will never see you as anything more than a childhood friend. Never!"

Vivienne stared at him, his words striking, like a slap to the face.

"Have some dignity," Dominic continued, his voice cold and unyielding. "Stop begging. It's beneath you."

Vivienne's eyes burned with hurt and fury, and she comprehended she had lost the battle. She turned and stormed out.

The air felt heavier with the tension Vivienne had stirred, refusing to dissipate. Dominic stood motionless, his fists still clenched, his breath coming in measured draws. Had he been too harsh? Perhaps. But Vivienne needed to hear the truth. Their connection was of the past, a bond that had long since outlived its purpose. The way she invoked Isabella's name, twisting it to fuel her own agenda, ignited a rage he couldn't suppress.

"Isabella." The pain of her loss was still raw, even after all this time. He had never truly grieved, instead, burying himself in work and distractions, building walls so high that even he couldn't scale them. But Vivienne's words had unearthed the guilt he carried that he could not save Isabella, that going forward felt like a betrayal.

He exhaled sharply, gripping the balcony railing. What am I doing? How did my life spiral into this mess? Haunted by the past, chasing after one woman, while being hounded by another?

His thoughts turned to the reason he had come out to the balcony. Danielle, with her calm fortitude and unshakable faith. She was everything his world lacked. Uncomplicated, pure, and grounded to the extent that it drew him in like a moth to a flame.

She made him feel alive again, but not in the reckless, fleeting way of his past relationships. With her, he felt the pull toward something deeper and lasting. But he also knew he wasn't ready. His grief, his insecurities, his fears. They were barriers he hadn't yet torn down.

Chapter 26

The words of a gossip are swallowed greedily and they go down into a person's innermost being.

-Proverbs 18:8

The following Monday, the communal area was alight with post-gala chatter. However, beneath the surface, something more insidious was brewing. Barbara, emboldened by her drunken conversation with Vivienne the night before, saw an opportunity to stir up trouble.

She had been waiting for an occasion to undermine Danielle and now, with the whispers of tension at the gala fresh in everyone's mind, the timing felt perfect.

"Well, I know why Danielle never joins us for drinks," she announced, her voice deliberately loud, ensuring her words carried across the group of women gathered near the coffee machine.

She smirked, pausing for effect. "She thinks she's too good for us. Probably because she's in bed with the boss and I mean *literally*."

A hush fell over the room before ripples of murmurs spread through the group. A few women exchanged glances, their intrigue piqued by Barbara's scandalous insinuation.

Emily, who had always admired Danielle for her professionalism and kindness, frowned and immediately stepped in.

"That's not true, Barbara," she said firmly. "Danielle doesn't come to drink because of her faith. She's a Christian."

Barbara snickered, clearly amused. "A Christian?" "Please!" she muttered with a roll of her eyes. "She's no saint. She walks around as if she's Miss Goody Two Shoes, but in truth, she's just another home-wrecker. Vivienne called me in tears last night. Apparently, Danielle's been cosying up to Dominic, acting all innocent while stealing her man."

The accusation hung in the air like a dark omen, and the ripple effect was immediate. Some women shifted uncomfortably, glancing down the hallway as if Danielle might walk in at any moment. Others leaned in, their expressions eager as Barbara's words validated the jealousy and suspicion they'd been harbouring.

"Well, I noticed Dominic paying her more attention than anyone else at the gala," responded a colleague.

"Exactly," Barbara interjected; her tone dripping with self-satisfaction. "She's not as innocent as she pretends to be."

"Barbara, that's enough!" "Spreading such rumours is unfair; we don't know the entire story."

"Oh, really? Do you believe you know better? I was there, Emily. I saw it all. Vivienne has been with Dominic for years. Then Danielle shows up, all wide-eyed and innocent, and suddenly she's catching his attention. Open your eyes!"

Emily exhaled sharply, her frustration obvious. "Rumours don't equal facts, Barbara. Danielle's never acted like she's above anyone here."

Barbara crossed her arms, leaning back smugly. "Believe what you want. I'm just saying you shouldn't be surprised when the truth comes out."

"Look, unless you have proof, we should stop dragging her name through the mud," Emily retorted.

Barbara smirked as she observed the ripple effect of her words permeate the group. It went beyond Danielle, though she'd never admit it. Barbara had spent years trying to climb the corporate ladder, only to watch someone like Danielle wak in with her perfect smile and impeccable record. It wasn't fair, and if Barbara had to knock her down a peg to feel better about herself, so be it.

Danielle stepped into the office canteen, arriving a little later than usual and immediately sensed a shift in the atmosphere.

The usual hum of conversation quieted ever so slightly, just enough for her to notice. Quick, fleeting glances were thrown her way, conversations pausing for a beat before resuming in hushed whispers.

It was subtle, but unmistakable. She was being talked about.

Her heart sank. Keeping her expression neutral, she grabbed a sandwich and a bottle of water and moved to the coffee machine, acutely aware of the stares following her.

Seated at a nearby table, Barbara leaned in close to a colleague, murmuring something that earned a stifled laugh. When Danielle glanced in their direction, Barbara smirked, holding her gaze for a beat before casually turning back to her conversation, a silent message that didn't need words.

Danielle's usual friendly colleagues seemed distant, their smiles faint, their greetings hesitant, as if unsure where they stood.

As she passed a group of women, snippets of their conversation reached her ears, "... gala, Vivienne, Dominic..."

Her stomach twisted. She sat at an empty table, forcing herself to take a bite of her sandwich. But the whispers continued, growing louder in her thoughts even as she tried to ignore them. Her appetite disappeared.

She couldn't take it anymore. She stood and made her way over to Emily, who she had spotted at the other side of the room. "Emily," she breathed, her voice composed but tinged with anxiety. "Can I talk to you for a minute?"

Emily looked at her group, hesitation flickering in her eyes, before nodding. "Sure, Danielle, let's step outside."

Once they were in a quiet corner outside the canteen, Danielle turned to Emily, her eyes full of concern. "What's going on? Why is everyone acting so weird?"

Emily hesitated, biting her lip. "Barbara has been spreading rumours."

Danielle's brow furrowed. "Rumours, about what?"

Emily glanced around, lowering her voice. "About you and Dominic. Apparently, Vivienne called Barbara, and she's accusing you of coming between them."

Danielle's eyes widened in disbelief. "What? That's ridiculous! None of that is true."

"I know, Danielle," Emily said quickly, her tone remorseful. "But Barbara's been telling everyone about Vivienne's version of events. That you're using your position to get close to Dominic."

Danielle gasped. The whispers, the stares, the coldness, it all made sense now. "What should I do?" she asked quietly.

Emily sighed, her expression sympathetic. "Keep your head up. The truth always comes out, eventually. People are going to talk, you can't stop that."

Danielle nodded, swallowing the tightness in her throat. "Thanks, Emily."

Danielle hurried back to her office, but the familiar space that once brought comfort now felt suffocating. She clenched her jaw, willing herself to stay composed. She had done nothing wrong, she knew that. But the whispers and sideways glances gnawed at her resolve. How much damage had already been done?

Chapter 27

The Lord is close to the broken-hearted and saves those who are crushed in spirit.

- Psalms 34:18

Danielle sat in front of her computer, staring blankly at her screen, the rows of numbers and words blurring into an incomprehensible haze. She could not focus. Her mind clouded by the tangled mess of the gala, the persistent rumours, and the emotional quagmire that was Dominic Pascale. Without saying goodbye, she packed her bag, keeping her head low, and left earlier than usual. Her feet moved mechanically as she proceeded to her jeep, her spirit utterly drained.

The drive home felt endless, each red light stretching time, each mile dragging under the weight of her thoughts. The steady hum of the engine and the blur of passing streetlights did little to quiet the storm churning inside her. By the time she finally pulled into her driveway, her grip on her composure was threadbare, unravelling with every shaky breath.

She entered her home, shutting the door, but the usual comfort of her space felt distant, almost alien. The walls appeared to converge, amplifying the noise in her head. Her bag slipped from her shoulder, landing in a forgotten heap by the door, as she drifted to the middle of the living room.

Her knees buckled, and she sank to the floor, her palms hitting the hardwood. Her breath came in shallow, uneven gasps as her eyes filled with tears. She attempted to hold them back, to keep the dam intact, but the pressure was too great. A sob escaped her lips, and then another. Soon, the tears spilled over, hot and unrelenting, soaking her cheeks as her shoulders trembled violently from grief.

"Oh God..." she whispered through her tears, her voice quivering and broken. "I don't have a clue what to do anymore." The words were a plea for a release of everything she'd been holding inside. Danielle buried her face in her palms, tears slipping through her fingers as she cried harder.

"Why is this happening to me? What is the reason behind my current emotions? Why do I care so much about him and what people are saying?" her voice cracked with anguish. "I just want to do what's right and follow you."

Her thoughts raced, colliding with each other like waves crashing against a shore. Her mind drifted to Dominic, the gravitation she felt towards him, how her heart seemed to betray her every time he was near. She thought of the rumours twisting her integrity into something vile, something she didn't recognise. It felt unfair, unbearable.

"I refuse this God," she shouted, her voice raw with desperation. "I refuse to feel this way about him and don't want to be caught in this mess. Please, assist me in discerning what you want for me."

She spoke with pain, her body trembling under the burden she alone shouldered. "I need you, your strength, your wisdom." "I feel so lost, so far from the path I'm supposed to be on. Instruct me on how to proceed."

Silence filled the room except for her ragged breaths and the soft crackle of the world settling around her. She pressed her cheek to the cool hardwood, her tears pooling beneath her, as her sobs gradually subsided into quiet sniffles. The silence stretched on, but it wasn't empty. It felt heavy with presence, as if the walls themselves were listening. Slowly, her breathing steadied, and a faint warmth spread through her chest. It wasn't peace, not yet, but it was the faintest hint of a whisper beyond her hearing.

Her lips moved again, a soft prayer escaping into the stillness. "Help me trust You, Lord," her voice shaking but resolute. "Because right now, you're all I have." And then, as if carried on by the breath of her surrender, came a still, small voice within her spirit, a quiet reassurance. *You are not alone. I am with you.*

Those words fell upon her like a gentle rain. She stayed there, her cheek against the floor, her heart still aching but a spark of hope kindling in the darkness. She lacked full understanding, but at long last, she felt the faintest assurance that she wasn't walking this path alone. "I'm thankful, Lord, for you not letting me go."

Danielle resolved to take one step at a time, trusting that clarity would come as she leaned on Christ, whose presence was unwavering. The storm within her had not yet abated, but she anchored herself in the promise that she was never alone. As she stood from the floor, her decision settled over her, a fragile yet comforting cloak of faith and resolve.

Across the city, another heart wrestled with its own turmoil, seeking solace in the company of his trusted friend. Although worlds apart, longing and uncertainty invisibly tied their paths together, each grappling with unanswerable questions.

The pair sat at their usual rooftop bar, the evening air cool, the city's gentle hum a distant murmur, enjoying the privacy of their tucked-away spot. The panorama of the city stretched out before them, lights twinkling in the distance, but Dominic was hardly paying attention.

His head was a swirling mess of thoughts and it didn't help that he hadn't been in the office today. He had to figure out what to do about about Danielle. Dominic felt Daze's careful scrutiny as he nursed his drink, waiting for him to say something. Dominic sighed "I'm at a loss, man."

"This about Vivienne or Danielle?"

Dominic let out a low, frustrated groan. "Both, I guess. Vivienne's completely losing it. She cornered me at the gala, rattling off a bunch of wild things, talking about Isabella, about how she's gone and never coming back."

His voice darkened, a mix of disbelief and frustration. "She's convinced we're meant to be together, like it's some twisted fate. And she's been trying to..." He exhaled sharply, shaking his head. "I don't know, claim me, like I'm some kind of prize she's entitled to."

"Yeah, I figured something like that was coming. She's been obsessed with you for years, Dom. But man, bringing up Isabella like that, that's low, even for her."

Dominic clenched his jaw, the sting of Vivienne's words still raw, festering beneath the surface. "She crossed a line," his voice taut with frustration. "She had no right."

"And you told her off, I hope?"

"I did," Dominic admitted, his voice edged with uncertainty. He leaned forward, resting his elbows on his knees, his fingers loosely clasped. His gaze drifted, unfocused. "But I feel like I may have been too harsh." He exhaled slowly, rubbing a hand over his face. "And then there's Danielle..."

Daze set his drink down, nodding knowingly. "Yeah. That's what this is really about, isn't it?"

"She told me she needs time. I understand, you know? I haven't been fair to her, but how much time should I give? How do I make her see I'm serious?"

Daze took a moment, his expression thoughtful as he considered his response. "You messed up, Dom," he said bluntly, though his tone was gentle. "Danielle's not like the women you've dated before. She's not playing games, she's serious about her beliefs, her values. Two weeks of silence: a major mistake, bro. It must have hurt her. If you care about her, you've gotta start there."

"I know. That's why I'm asking. I don't want to rush her, but I don't want to lose her either."

"Look, you've got to respect what she's asked for. Give her the space she needs, but that doesn't mean you disappear entirely. Just don't crowd her, but don't vanish either. Show her you respect her boundaries, but still care. Let her come to you when she's ready."

Daze studied his brother his tone uncharacteristically serious. "Dom, let me ask you something. Are you ready for this? I'm not talking about whether you want her. I mean, are you prepared to be the man she needs, because if you're not, you may do more harm than good."

Dominic pondered the question. "I have no idea, but I can't just walk away. I refuse to," he admitted finally.

Daze concurred with a nod. "Then figure it out. Fast. Because Danielle doesn't seem like a woman who waits forever. Show her why she shouldn't let you go, either. Right now, she's scared, hurt and probably wondering if you're someone she can depend on. You've got to prove you are and Dom, that doesn't happen overnight."

"The issue is, I don't know if I can do this the right way," he said after a long pause. "I've never felt like this before and have no clue what to do."

Daze chuckled softly. "That's because this isn't like anything you've ever dealt with before. Danielle's different. She's making you work for it and honestly, that's a good thing. It means she's serious about you. Now you have to decide if you're willing to put in the effort to show her you're serious, too."

"I am. I just don't know how to make her believe it."

"Slowly but surely, brother. Start by being her ideal man, not the one you've always been. She'll see the difference, eventually."

"Thanks, man," he said, giving Daze a small, appreciative nod.

"Hey, that's what I'm here for." Daze grinned, raising his glass. "Now let's drink before you cry." Dominic chuckled despite himself, lifting his glass.

The following day, Dominic sat in his office, reviewing reports, when he heard a knock. Without looking up, he called out, "Come in."

The door opened and Andre stepped in, his expression unusually tense.

"Sir," Andre began, standing just inside the door, "there's something I must bring to your attention."

His assistant's unease immediately set off alarm bells. Dominic lowered his report, then saw Andre, usually composed, now visibly flustered.

"What is it, Andre?"

Andre stepped closer, lowering his voice slightly. "There's some gossip going around the office, sir. It's about you and Danielle."

Dominic's eyes narrowed instantly. This direction displeased him. Andre shifted, clearly uncomfortable. "Apparently, someone's been spreading rumours that you and Danielle are involved in a relationship. That she's come between you and Vivienne."

Dominic stared at Andre, the words sinking in, and then anger flickered within his expression.

"Andre, who started this?"

Andre shook his head. "I haven't found out yet, but it's spreading fast. A few people overheard it in the communal area yesterday and from what I've heard, it's already reached several departments. The ladies were talking about it at lunch."

Dominic's hands clenched into fists. He felt not just anger, but rage. This exceeded simple gossip; it was a direct attack on Danielle's reputation and character.

"And they're dragging Danielle into this filth?" Memories of her unwavering professionalism, her gentle resilience, and the pain she must be trying so hard to hide flared in his thoughts. "After everything she's done to maintain her integrity, they have the audacity to slander her?"

Andre nodded. "From what I understand, it's gaining traction and people are doubting her integrity."

Dominic stood abruptly, his chair scraping across the floor. How much of this was his fault? His protracted period of quiet, the tension at the gala. It was like leaving an open door for gossip to slither through.

"Find out who started this," Dominic snapped, his voice razor-sharp. "I don't care how long it takes or who's involved. I want names."

"I'll get on it immediately, sir."

Dominic started pacing. He'd spent years building a reputation as an unflinching leader, but this was different. Danielle's dignity was being dragged through the mud and despite not being his to defend, he felt an unshakable responsibility to shield her from this.

"Andre," he said, halting mid-stride, his tone softening but still intense. "Make sure Danielle doesn't hear about this until it's handled."

Andre hesitated. "I think it's already too late for that," he admitted quietly, before stepping out.

Dominic froze. The thought of Danielle enduring the whispers, the judgment, it stung sharper than he'd expected. He slumped into his chair, staring at the door Andre had just closed, a single thought rang loud and clear - *This stops now.*

Chapter 28

"It is an honour for a person to keep away from strife, but every fool will be quarrelling."

-Proverbs 20:3

Towards the close of the day, Danielle sat at her desk, staring at her computer screen, when her phone rang. It was Dominic.

She hesitated before answering. "Hello, Dominic."

"Danielle, I know you've asked for space, and I'm trying to respect that, but I've heard about the rumours, and I felt I should let you know I'm handling it."

She suspected the rumours might have reached Dominic, but hearing his voice only made it harder to keep her emotions in check. "Dominic," she began with a sigh, "you shouldn't get involved. That will only exacerbate the situation. If you step in, people will speculate even more."

"No," he interrupted, his tone firm but not harsh. "I can't stand by and let them tarnish your name. This isn't something you should have to shoulder alone. You've done nothing wrong, Danielle."

Her voice softened, though her resolve remained. "I appreciate that, but you know how these things works. If you intervene, it'll only confirm what people are whispering about. The more attention we give it, the worse it gets."

Dominic exhaled sharply, his frustration palpable. "So, I'm supposed to stand back while they drag your reputation through the mud?"

"They're not lies exactly," Danielle said quietly, her words measured and heavy. "They're twisted versions of what could become truth if we're not careful. Even if nothing happened, people will talk. The best thing we can do is let it blow over."

Silence stretched on the other end, and Danielle could imagine him pacing, trying to reign in his instinct to fix things. His voice raw, he finally admitted, "I don't like this, Danielle, and I hate that you're being dragged into something you didn't ask for. I must protect you."

Her heart clenched in response to his utterance, a longing she tried to suppress stirring deep within her. "I know," she whispered, "but if you really want to protect me, you'll let me handle this my way. Please. I can't have you fighting my battles. It will just complicate matters."

Another pause. She could almost hear the battle between his protective nature and his deference to her wishes. "Alright," he said, reluctantly. "I'll back off for now. But if this gets worse, Danielle, I won't just stand by. Understood?"

"Yes," she replied, her voice heavy with gratitude and weariness. "Thanks for caring, really."

"Always," he responded tenderly. "If you need anything—no matter what. Call me."

"I will." "Goodnight, Dominic."

"Goodnight, Danielle."

Thursday afternoon, Danielle had just left a tense meeting. She was walking towards the elevator when Barbara obstructed her path, her arms crossed.

"Danielle, we have to talk," Barbara said, her tone sharp, stopping Danielle in her tracks.

Danielle inhaled, steadying herself. She had a sinking feeling this conversation was long overdue. "Barbara, I doubt this is the time or place."

Barbara stepped closer and lowered her voice. "Oh, I think it is. You've got everyone fooled, haven't you? Little Miss Innocent. But I see through all of it."

Danielle's eyes narrowed. "I am uncertain what you think you see, Barbara, but I have done nothing wrong. Whatever rumours are going around, they're not true."

"Really?" Barbara scoffed, crossing her arms tighter. "Is that what you tell yourself to make you feel better? You profess to be a Christian, yet you're busy stealing other people's man. You're a harlot!"

Danielle experienced a surge of anger, but fought to stay composed. "I am not in Dominic's life the way you think. And if you choose to spread lies about me, that's on you, but I will not engage with it. Precisely what are you trying to accomplish by doing this?"

Barbara's eyes flashed and in that instant, Danielle thought she saw vulnerability, behind the hostility. Then Barbara took another step forward, her voice quieter, more intense.

"You don't get it, do you? I worked my way up from nothing. Grew up in an estate with an abusive father who took everything from me: my self-esteem, my sense of safety. I clawed my way out of that hell, studied harder than anyone because I had to. I was forced to be perfect."

Danielle blinked, taken aback by Barbara's confession, but remained silent.

Barbara's voice cracked slightly, but she kept going, her words spilling out. "I've sacrificed everything for this job, for my future here. I've done what it takes to get ahead and now you haven't been here half as long, coming and ruining the status quo. You act, all holier-than-thou, acting like you're above all of us. Like you're untouchable. You're a threat to everything I've built."

"A threat?" Danielle repeated, her tone incredulous. "Barbara, I've never once tried to undermine you or anyone else. I came here to work, to fulfill my duties, just like you. If you believe I'm your rival, you're mistaken."

Barbara's jaw clenched. "You don't understand. The issue isn't what you did. It's about who you are. People like you glide through life, everything handed to you, because you're perceived to be at a disadvantage! People like me must struggle every inch. I can't afford to let anyone get in my way, including you!"

Danielle's heart ached as she listened, realising that Barbara's aggression extended beyond her. It was about years of pain and fear that had twisted into resentment.

"I'm sorry for what you went through, but bullying won't secure your place here, Barbara. If anything, it's going to undermine everything you've worked for. And contrary to what you believe, I earned everything myself, pushing through discrimination, skepticism, you name it to get here."

Barbara's mouth contorted into a bitter smile. "Maybe. But I refuse to sit back and let you come in and take what I've earned. I have a plan for my life here at Pascale & Pascale. A plan that doesn't include anyone stepping into my path."

Danielle met Barbara's gaze without flinching, her voice unwavering. "You can't control people by tearing them down, Barbara. Whatever you've been through, it doesn't justify this behaviour. You're only hurting yourself the most. Don't you see that? The fulfilment you're searching for isn't in power or control, it's in healing, and that can only come from God. If you're open to it, I would be happy to pray with you. He can heal your pain, if you let Him."

There was a softness in Danielle's tone, an offer of grace, a quiet hope that Barbara might choose a different path. Barbara's face twisted, a blend of anger and what looked like regret flashed across her features. For an instant, Danielle thought she might soften just enough to hear her out. But Barbara turned sharply, her shoulders stiff with defiance.

"I don't need a lecture from you, or your sanctimonious prayer," Barbara spat, her words dripping with contempt. "Just stay out of my way." and with that, she stormed off.

Danielle stood frozen, watching Barbara's retreating figure with a deep sadness. Why did it have to come to this? Women should uplift each other, not tear each other down.

By Friday, Danielle was physically, mentally, and emotionally drained. When a text from Dominic came through asking her to meet for dinner on Saturday, she surprised herself by saying yes. For once, she desired to step out of the storm and reclaim a sliver of control.

Chapter 29

"Ah, stubborn children," declared the Lord, who carry out a plan, but not mine, and who make an alliance, but not of my Spirit, that they may add sin to sin.

-Isaiah 30:1

Saturday night arrived and Danielle stood before her mirror, assessing her reflection with admiration and defiance. The wide-leg jumpsuit she chose was a rich burnt orange, a colour that complemented her warm skin tone and brought out the amber flecks of her eyes.

The fabric draped elegantly, cinching at the waist with a sleek belt and skimming her figure without being overly revealing. Its V-neckline hinted at sophistication rather than provocation, and the tailored shoulders added a sharp, confident edge. Delicate gold earrings and nude heels completed the look, striking the perfect balance between bold and refined.

Tonight isn't about them, she thought, adjusting her gold earrings one last time. *It's about me. If they want to talk, let them. I'll show them I'm unshaken.*

When Dominic, his reaction was instant and unguarded. His eyes lit up, his gaze sweeping over her with unmistakable appreciation, his mouth forming a slow, approving smile.

Danielle was mesmerised by his effortless charm. He carried a level of sophistication in his attire, balancing casually polished in a way, only he could. A white T-shirt fit snugly across his broad chest, accompanied by a striking gold chain that peeked from beneath the neckline. Over it, he wore a black and grey blazer with a subtle herringbone pattern, the tailored fit highlighting his strong shoulders.

His black jeans, dark and immaculately pressed, tapered perfectly to reveal sleek black leather shoes polished to a shine. The gold accents against the monochromatic ensemble lending him an understated elegance.

"You've outdone yourself," he whispered, his tone carrying an edge of reverence.

A warmth spread across Danielle's neck. "Thank you. You dress down well."

Dominic chuckled softly, opening the car door with a graceful gesture. "I'll take that as a compliment. Ready to go?"

Danielle nodded, climbing into the car.

Dominic's car was a sleek, black Aston Martin DB11, an embodiment of luxury and power. The polished exterior gleamed, its aerodynamic curves exuding elegance and performance. With its front signature grille and narrow, sharp LED headlights, it resembled a predator about to pounce.

It sat low to the ground on pristine alloy wheels, their intricate design adding a hint of artistry to its muscular frame. Inside, the cabin was just as impressive, a fusion of craftsmanship and technology. Smooth leather seats, stitched with precision, embraced the driver and passengers in comfort, while the dashboard, finished in brushed aluminum and glossy black accents, housed a state-of-the-art entertainment system.

As Danielle settled into the passenger seat, the soft scent of leather and Dominic's cologne filled the air. The ambient lighting bathed the interior in a subtle glow. When Dominic started the engine, the deep, throaty purr of the V12 reverberated through the night, a testament to the car's raw power.

"It suits you," Danielle remarked.

Dominic eyed her, a smile tugging at the corner of his lips. "You think so?" he asked, shifting into gear with a practised ease.

"Yes, but I'll reserve judgment until I see how you handle it."

He laughed, the sound low and rich. "Buckle up, Miss Thompson. Let's find out."

This man is trouble, she thought. Though she wasn't quite able to bring herself to mind. Tonight was hers to own, rumours be damned.

As the Aston Martin glided effortlessly through the city streets, the soulful strains of old-school R&B wrapped around them, an unspoken presence neither acknowledged aloud. Yet, in the quiet, the tension hummed—her slightly quickened breath, his grip tightening just a fraction on the steering wheel—a silent understanding.

The velvet voices of Marvin Gaye, Al Green, and Anita Baker wove through the air, their timeless melodies filling the space. Danielle gazed through the window, watching the city lights blur into streaks of gold and white. The tension from the week ebbed away, giving way to a cautious anticipation.

Dominic broke the silence. "Do you mind the music?"

"Not at all. I didn't peg you for an R&B fan, though."

He chuckled, his fingers tapping softly on the wheel in time with the beat. "There's much you don't know about me, Miss Thompson."

"Oh? Is that a challenge, Mr Pascale?"

He directed a sidelong glance at her, his smile deepening. "Perhaps."

Their conversation tapered off, giving way to a comfortable silence as the music took centre stage once more. The rich tones of a Luther Vandross ballad wrapped around them, the lyrics almost mirroring the unspoken thoughts that swirled between them.

Dominic drove the Aston Martin smoothly into the driveway of an upscale restaurant. It hinted at exclusivity. As Dominic parked, he cut the engine and turned to Danielle.

"I hope you're hungry."

"Starving," she drawled as she accepted his hand, stepping out of the car into the evening air. The place was an intimate, richly decorated and secluded space, precisely the atmosphere Dominic wanted. He chose a table near a window where they could talk without interruptions.

"This is beautiful," Danielle said as they sat down, glancing around the restaurant.

"Yes, it is," Dominic said, his gaze settling on her, the intensity in his eyes making it clear he wasn't just talking about the restaurant.

"So, what did you think of the gala, apart from well, all the drama it seems to have sparked," asked Dominic smiled wryly, swirling his glass of wine as he observed her.

Danielle chuckled softly. "The gala itself was beautiful. I enjoyed the music and the setting, but I didn't expect to end up the subject of office speculation because of it."

Dominic was so impressed by her self-deprecating response, he couldn't help asked, "How do you stay so calm? There's something about you that makes it seem like you would stay steady even if the world collapsed."

"I wouldn't say I'm always calm, but my faith plays a big role in that. It helps me stay grounded when things feel chaotic."

With genuine curiosity, he commented, "Your faith. You've mentioned it before. It seems unshakable. How do you hold on to it so tightly?"

Danielle's eyes lit up as she spoke. "It's not always easy, but it's what gives me peace and purpose. I believe that irrespective of what happens, there's a plan, and that trust keeps me steady. It's an unshakeable foundation."

Dominic studied her. "I admire that. I doubt I've ever had that kind of certainty about anything."

Danielle smiled gently, leaning forward slightly. "Certainty isn't always about knowing everything. Sometimes it's just about trusting in what you can't see."

"I think I've spent so much of my life trying to control outcomes I've forgotten how to trust anything beyond my grasp. If I can't shape it, predict it, or steer it, it feels... uncertain. And letting go of that? It's harder than I'd like to admit."

Danielle regarded him. "It's not something you find overnight, but it's worth the search."

Danielle wavered, her fingers lightly tracing the rim of her coffee cup as she gathered her thoughts. The question had been on her mind for a while now and despite her uncertainty, the conversation felt like the right moment. "You never told me about your beliefs, Dominic. I know it's a strange question, but my faith is a big part of who I am, as you've alluded to. Do you believe in God?"

Following a lengthy silence, he spoke, his voice more vulnerable than she'd ever heard it. "I haven't figured out where I stand, honestly," he confessed. "I've heard about God and my mom took me to church when I was younger, but as I grew older, I started questioning. If God exists, where was He when my father nearly destroyed me? Where was He when I lost Isabella?"

At his mention of Isabella, his tone softened, and Danielle noticed she clearly still held a powerful grip on Dominic's heart. The world outside seemed to fall away and only the rawness of Dominic's pain remained, swirling between them.

Danielle said nothing, allowing him the space to continue. Dominic's eyes met hers, his expression tinged with the frustration he carried.

"I've witnessed so much suffering, so much cruelty. If there's a God, why does He let allow all of it? What's the purpose of all the pain? I don't know whether I can believe in a God who would allow that. The suffering I've seen is senseless." His voice broke slightly on the last sentence, betraying the exhaustion in his soul.

She wanted to extend a hand, to offer comfort, but she chose her words carefully. "I don't have all the answers, Dominic, but I believe there's always a reason behind the pain, even if we don't see it right away."

"It shapes us and prepares us for things we don't understand until later. Even in the darkest moments, God is there, even if it doesn't seem like it. He doesn't abandon us, even when we feel most alone."

"As for your question on why He allows it? He doesn't. The gift of free will grants us the freedom and power to make choices for good or evil."

"The suffering in the world is not a manifestation of God's will but the consequence of human beings choosing cruelty, selfishness and a path that often strays far from Him."

"If we truly embraced His commandment to love one another to show compassion, kindness and understanding, so much of the pain we see would cease to exist. It's not God who abandons us; it's us that often abandons Him."

Dominic's eyes softened, and he gave the impression of taking in her words slowly, as though they were a lifeline thrown into the deep waters he'd been struggling to stay afloat in. He exhaled slowly, his gaze turning inward.

"I'm uncertain I'm willing to believe that. It seems like too much to ask.

Danielle's voice softened as she met Dominic's gaze, her expression sincere but gentle. "Have you tried reaching out to God, Dominic?" "You've been bearing all this pain on your own, but have you really given Him a chance? Have you reached out to Him, even in your doubt?"

She paused, giving him time to absorb the questions. "I know it's hard, but He's here, waiting for you. You've given up on Him without asking for help. How is this fair? He says in His Word that if we call upon His name, He will hear us and give us rest, but we first have to cast all our burdens upon Him."

Danielle continued filled with a quiet conviction. "Faith doesn't erase pain, but helps you carry it and isn't concerned with instant answers; it's about trust."

Dominic rubbed his neck, a gesture Danielle hadn't seen from him before. It was small, almost imperceptible, but it spoke volumes.

"I don't know whether I can just let go like that," he admitted, his eyes flicking to the floor as if ashamed. "I've been holding on to hurt, the confusion, anger for so long, letting it all go and trusting someone I can't see is terrifying."

"There's a part of me that wants to believe, but I'm not ready yet, but I hear what you're saying. I'll think about it, Danielle. Thank you."

"All I ask is that you keep an open heart, Dominic. Sometimes, that's all it takes for God to work on your behalf."

As the conversation waned, a serene silence settled between them, the soft clink of cutlery against plates easing the tension that had settled around their table.

Dominic swirled the last sip of wine in his glass, measuring his next words carefully before finally making eye contact. "I have a business trip to Paris next week," he said casually, but with clear intent. "You're fluent in French, and I was hoping you could accompany me. It would be beneficial for the company."

Danielle's eyebrows lifted in surprise. She could see through the pretense instantly. This exceeded business, and they both knew it. Her logical side implored her to decline, to avoid stepping further into the web of complications already surrounding them. Don't do it, Danielle. This is risky, too risky.

But there it was again, the quiet defiance, the spark of rebellion she couldn't fully extinguish since the rumours started. It defied her better judgment, whispering that she could handle this, that she deserved to reclaim some control over her own narrative.

She nodded slowly, the decision surprising even for her. "All right, I'll come." Dominic smiled wide. "Good. I'll make the arrangements."

With the evening's end approaching, Dominic offered to drop her home, but Danielle declined. "Thank you, but I'll take a cab."

He hesitated, but he respected her decision. "All right."

Danielle smiled, appreciating the gesture. She called for a cab and after a quick goodbye, she slid into the cab and as it wound through the quiet streets, and rested her head against the cool glass. Later that night, Danielle sat alone as she held a warm mug of tea, her gaze distant as her mind sifted through the evening's events.

She replayed his words, his hesitant confession of doubt, and the vulnerability he had permitted her to see. It was unexpected—the depth of pain beneath his confident facade. He wasn't just the enigmatic, commanding man she saw at work. There was more to him, layers shaped by loss, anger and the absence of answers he desperately sought.

His struggles resonated with her to some extent. She understood doubt, the moments when faith resembled a thin thread, barely keeping one tethered. But what stayed with her, what offered her a sliver of hope, was that Dominic hadn't dismissed God outright.

He wasn't a staunch unbeliever or closed off to the idea of faith. His questions weren't rejections; they were cries for understanding. Somewhere beneath the hurt, she saw it—a spark of curiosity, a yearning for something more, even if he couldn't name it yet.

There's hope, she thought, setting the mug down, her eyes drifted toward the ceiling as a sigh escaped her lips. Maybe he's not as far from God as he thinks. Maybe, in time, I could help him see the light.

The thought was both thrilling and daunting. She knew the risks, the potential for heartbreak, the danger of placing too much hope in someone still wrestling with their demons. And yet, her heart was compelled to hold on to the possibility.

If Dominic could come to know Christ, if he could truly surrender his pain and find peace, their future together wouldn't just be a dream, it could be something lasting, something divinely orchestrated.

She also knew, however, she had to be careful. This wasn't just about her feelings; it was about her convictions, her faith, and the boundaries she'd promised herself she wouldn't cross. This was delicate—a balance between patience and hope, between wanting to guide him and knowing she couldn't be his saviour. Only God could do that.

Lord, she prayed silently, her hands clasping together, please guide me. Show me how to navigate this. Help me trust in your timing and your will. And please help Dominic find his way to You. Heal his heart and let him see the peace that only you can give.

She exhaled, her heart lighter than before, as if her prayer had lifted some of the burden from her shoulders. For now, all she could do was wait and trust that God's plan, whatever it was, would unfold as it should. And trust herself to be patient, even when her heart longed to rush ahead. With that, she surrendered the night and all its questions to God, who held every solution.

Chapter 30

"Listen to advice and accept discipline, and at the end you will be counted among the wise."

-Proverbs 19:20

Sunday after church, Danielle sat across from Naomi and Ten in their beloved café. Sunlight poured in from the large panes of glass, bathing their table in a golden glow.

Freshly brewed coffee mingled with the sweet scent of vanilla from a nearby pastry case created a warmth that belied the charged atmosphere at their table. The murmur of discussions and the clinking of cups faded into the background as Danielle shared her heart.

"So, that was my week," Danielle said, finishing her story with a sigh. She stared into her coffee. "And I've agreed to go to Paris with Dominic." Her voice was steady, yet she couldn't meet her friends' eyes.

Naomi's head shot up, her brow furrowing. "Wait, wait, wait! You're sharing all this drama about Barbara, the work rumours, and now you're planning a trip with the man at the centre of it? Dani, you know I love you, but girl, what are you thinking?" Naomi leaned back, her expression shifting from confusion to exasperation.

Ten, ever the calm but firm voice of reason, leaned forward in disbelief. "Dani, you have consistently been so clear about your boundaries. You didn't marry Carter, although he was a bona fide Christian, because his family values didn't align with yours. And Dominic? He's not even sure if he believes in God. How is this different? What's changed?"

Danielle's stomach churned. She knew they were right, but hearing it aloud from her closest friends made her decision feel even more precarious. "I know," she admitted quietly. "I'm not sure what I'm doing either. It's just with Dominic, it feels different. He's not rejecting God outright. He's searching, hurting. Maybe I can help him?"

Naomi groaned, pressing a hand to her forehead. "Danielle, we've been friends long enough for me to know your heart. You always want to help people. But you can't save someone's soul. That's between them and God. Remember Philippians 2:12—*work out your own salvation with fear and trembling.* He has to figure this out for himself."

Naomi's mention of Philippians 2:12 lingered in Danielle's mind. Work out your salvation with fear and trembling. Wasn't that exactly what she was supposed to be doing? And here she was, stepping into unknown waters, her heart leading her where her mind hesitated to follow.

Danielle's chest tightened as Naomi spoke, each word like a mirror reflecting the doubts she'd been too afraid to face. She wanted to believe that her affection for Dominic wasn't misplaced, that God's hand was in this. But as Ten's voice rose with concern, she wondered if she was allowing her emotions to cloud her judgment.

Ten nodded, her gaze unwavering. "You're a woman who loves God, Dani. You need a partner who's on that same journey. How do you reconcile that with someone who's still figuring out what he believes?"

Danielle bit her lip, her emotions swirling. "I know what I've said before, and I still believe it. But Dominic's different. He's been through so much pain. He's not closing the door on God, he's just lost and maybe God put me in his life to help guide him. Is that so wrong?"

Naomi's expression softened. "It's not wrong to care, Danielle. But don't forget, your relationship with God comes first. You've dedicated yourself to stay true to your beliefs. This situation? It's already messy. If Dominic never fully believes, can you really see a future with him?"

Danielle sat back, Naomi's question similar to the one that had haunted her nights, the one she couldn't answer. "I don't know," she admitted. "I'm not considering marriage, just taking things slowly. Maybe this trip will show me what God really wants for me."

Ten sighed, leaning forward. "We're not judging you, Dani. We're just worried. If marriage isn't on your mind, what's the point? You've said yourself that you are loath to compromise. Don't let him be the thing that makes you start."

Danielle looked at both her buddies, her chest tightening. Although she knew they were correct, the pull toward Dominic was something she couldn't explain or ignore. "I hear you, I really do, but I need to see where this goes, even if it's just to get some clarity."

Naomi bridged the gap across the table, squeezing Danielle's hand. "We'll be here for you, regardless. Just promise us you'll keep praying about this. Don't lose yourself in trying to help someone else, or worse, lose your soul."

Danielle nodded, her eyes stinging with unshed tears. "I promise."

As they remained quiet for a short time, Danielle's thoughts churned. She realised she was walking a fine line. Her faith was her anchor, but Dominic stirred a longing in her she couldn't disregard. But she resolved to keep praying, for guidance, lucidity, and most of all, for the strength to do what was right.

Chapter 31

For it is an act of righteousness on God's part to give trouble as their reward to those who are troubling you.

-2 Thessalonians 1:6

Dominic stood in his usual spot by the floor-to-ceiling windows of his office, watching the city move below him. Cars crawled through the streets, people hurried along sidewalks, all of it looking small from the 16th floor.

Why couldn't life be simpler? The thought remained, but there was no answer—just the steady hum of traffic in the distance. Without turning around, he spoke, his voice calm but expectant. "Have you found what I asked for?"

"Yes, Mr Pascale. Barbara started the rumours. I've compiled her work history, performance reviews, and flagged a few incidents from the past. While nothing major stands out on the surface, there's a pattern of manipulation. I've also gathered statements from colleagues who've had issues with her. We can build a strong case," reported Andre.

Dominic finally turned to face his assistant, his expression cold and unyielding. "Good. I want everything documented, including her involvement in these rumours. I won't allow her to poison this workplace any longer. If there's any more dirt to dig up, find it."

"Understood, Mr Pascale. I'll get everything ready."

"Thanks, Andre. Schedule a senior team meeting for this afternoon. I must address this and a few other matters."

A few hours later, the senior team gathered in the boardroom, murmurs of curiosity filling the space. Barbara sat in her usual spot, her posture confident, though her fingers fidgeted beneath the table.

She scanned the room, trying to read the mood, her anxiety masked by a practiced air of authority.

Dominic strode and his gaze swept over the team, pausing briefly on Barbara before moving on.

"First, I want to make it clear that gossip and slander have no place in this company. We operate with professionalism, integrity, and respect. Anyone found undermining these values will face swift consequences."

Barbara's stomach churned. His pronouncement was directed at everyone, but she knew it was specific to her. She forced her expression to remain neutral.

"Second," Dominic continued, his tone shifting slightly, "I will go to France later this week to complete a critical deal and Ms Thompson will accompany me." The room stilled, and Barbara's knuckles whitened as she clutched the armrests of her chair. Dominic's gaze flickered toward her, a subtle warning behind his gaze.

"Her skills make her the best choice for this assignment," he said firmly, brooking no opposition. "I expect full cooperation from everyone."

Barbara's mask of composure faltered. She managed a tight smile, her voice brittle as she said, "Of course, Mr Pascale. But surely, there are others more qualified? Danielle's role—"

"I'm well aware of everyone's roles," Dominic interrupted, his voice cold. "And I've made my decision."

The others noticed Barbara's challenge, but Dominic didn't allow her to push further. He redirected his focus back to the team, outlining the tasks and responsibilities for the coming days while he was away.

When the meeting concluded, Dominic remained seated at the head of the table, his focus unwavering. Meanwhile, Barbara lingered outside the boardroom, her mind racing with frustration and desperation. She wasn't willing to let the day end without having her say.

Barbara knew she was taking a risk as she made her way back to the boardroom. She had ascended to her position through sheer determination, and now, in one swift move, it felt as though Danielle was being handed everything she had worked for. The sting of humiliation from the meeting burned within her.

She felt a surge of adrenaline as she finally pushed the door open. Dominic looked up, his face inscrutable. Barbara's heartbeat thundered in her ears as Dominic's cold, unwavering gaze pinned her in place.

"Barbara, what now?"

She feigned a smile. "I simply wanted to clarify if Danielle going to France—"

"Barbara," Dominic interrupted, his tone razor-sharp. "This isn't up for discussion. I made my decision based on her qualifications. That's the end of it."

Barbara hesitated, but pushed forward. "But with the rumours circulating, don't you think it sends the wrong message?"

Dominic stood, his movements deliberate and menacing. "The only wrong message is being sent by you, Barbara. I know you're behind the gossip."

Barbara's composure cracked. "Dominic, I—"

Dominic's gaze bore into her, his tone quiet yet cutting. "Barbara, let me reiterate. This company thrives because it operates on integrity and professionalism. What you've done undermines both. If you're incapable of understanding that, then you don't belong here."

He advanced with a growl. "And if you believe for one second I won't act, you're gravely mistaken. You've crossed a line, and this is your last warning. One more incident, and you're out. Do I make myself clear?"

Barbara swallowed hard, nodding tightly, knowing she'd pushed too far.

"Understood."

"Good. Get out."

Barbara's pulse thudded in her ears, her mind raced through possibilities, each one more spiteful than the last. If Dominic wanted to protect Danielle, he'd have to do better than that. Others underestimated her before, and she survived. This time would be no different.

Chapter 32

"Above all else, guard your heart, for everything you do flows from it."

-Proverbs 4:23

Danielle and Dominic arrived at the airport with time to spare. For Danielle, this trip to Paris wasn't only a professional milestone, it was a step into unfamiliar territory. The idea of being alone with Dominic for an extended period stirred feelings of anticipation and unease, emotions she was determined to keep in check.

The first-class treatment was seamless: priority check-in, expedited security, and the sanctuary of a private lounge. It was almost overwhelming, a sharp contrast to Danielle's simple living. She focused instead on her role, mentally running through the presentation she had prepared.

"I've made sure you've got everything you need for the meeting. The presentation will flow naturally, and your French will help smooth over any bumps."

Danielle smiled appreciatively. "Thank you. I've rehearsed it several times, but it's reassuring to hear you have confidence in me."

"Total confidence! I wouldn't have asked you to come if I thought otherwise. Of course, it doesn't hurt that I get to spend some time with you without the office politics," he cheekily replied.

"Careful, Mr Pascale. You sound overly confident."

He chuckled softly, his gaze steady. "Maybe I am."

The first-class cabin was a world of quiet luxury. Plush, reclining seats made Danielle feel that she'd stepped into another realm. She adjusted awkwardly, trying to mask her discomfort, whilst Dominic sat beside her with practiced ease.

"I've arranged for a driver when we land," Dominic said. "We'll go straight to the hotel. You'll have some time to yourself before dinner and tomorrow's meeting."

"That sounds perfect," Danielle replied, keeping her tone professional. "I'll use the time to polish the presentation."

Dominic nodded. "It's solid already. Just remember, they value relationships just as much as the numbers."

"So, charm them first, then dazzle them with my charts?"

"Exactly." Dominic's grin was easy, his gaze fixed on her before he shifted his attention back to his tablet.

As the plane soared into the clouds, exhaustion from the week settled over Danielle, her eyes growing heavy despite her best efforts to stay awake. Her head tilted to the side, coming to rest lightly on Dominic's shoulder.

Dominic stiffened slightly, surprised by the unexpected contact. His gaze dropped, finding her nestled against him, fast asleep, her breathing steady, her features softened in repose.

He let himself linger in the quiet intimacy of the moment, his eyes tracing the elegant lines of her face—the high cheekbones, the almond-shaped eyes, the fullness of her lips. She was breathtaking, and for a fleeting second, he basked in the thought that she felt safe enough to let her guard down around him completely.

But then a memory surfaced. Isabella. Her head had once rested against his shoulder just like this on a flight to Italy, her laughter light and unguarded, still echoing somewhere in the depths of his mind. The recollection struck like a sudden jolt of turbulence, tightening his chest. He looked away, swallowing hard, the past and present colliding, leaving him unsteady.

He didn't move her, though. Instead, he let her sleep, shielding her from the world, if only for a short time. With the airplane beginning its descent, Danielle stirred, blinking awake. She lifted her head and realised where she had been resting, her cheeks flushing in embarrassment.

"Oh, Dominic, I'm so sorry," she said, sitting up straight. "I didn't mean to..."

Dominic shrugged, offering her a reassured smile. "It's fine, Danielle. You needed the rest."

Danielle smiled gratefully, though her heart pounded a little from the brief intimacy. She glanced through the window, Paris coming into view below them. "It's beautiful."

"It is. Welcome to Paris."

The sleek black car glided through the vibrant streets of Paris, the city's iconic charm greeting them with every turn. Their hotel was breathtaking. With its blend of classic French architecture and modern sophistication, it stood as a symbol of Parisian luxury. As they stepped inside, the marble floors gleamed under the luxurious lighting. Danielle marvelled as they were escorted to their private suites on the top floor.

Her room was a dream of cream and gold, with plush furnishings and a terrace that offered an unobstructed glimpse of the Eiffel Tower. Briefly, she allowed herself to breathe, letting the beauty of the moment sink in. She bowed her head and prayed quietly.

"Lord, I'm thankful you've brought us here safely. Please guide my steps and keep me grounded. Let me reflect your grace, even in unfamiliar circumstances. Amen."

After a luxurious bath, Danielle wrapped herself in the softest towel she'd ever touched, the scent of lavender still clinging to her skin. The soft knock on the door startled her. She hesitated, her heart fluttering.

When she opened the door, Dominic stood on the other side. His gaze locked onto hers for a beat before dipping lower, sweeping over her towel-clad figure. The plush white towel hugged her curves, and she felt the weight of his gaze like a physical touch. His expression shifted, his eyes darkened, surprise and passion simmering in their depths. The air between them crackled.

He swallowed hard, his Adam's apple bobbing visibly. "I'm heading to my meeting," he said, his voice rougher than intended. His gaze flickered over her once more before he forced himself to look away. "I'll pick you up at 8:00 p.m. for dinner. The restaurant's nearby." The words were clipped, controlled—but the tension in his stance betrayed the effort it took to say them. Danielle's heart raced as she nodded. "Okay, thank you."

Before she could close the door, he bent down, brushing a light kiss against her cheek. "We're in France," he remarked with a teasing smile. "Kisses are cultural."

She froze, her skin tingling where his lips had touched. Dominic departed, his casual confidence leaving a trail of electricity in his wake. With a click, Danielle shut the door, her mind racing. The verse from *James 4:7* popped into her head: *Submit yourselves to God. Resist the devil, and he will flee from you. You know better than this. You're supposed to be representing Christ. What are you doing allowing yourself to get so close?*

But another insistent voice whispered in her thoughts. *Well, I'm not doing anything wrong, am I? It's just a business trip. It's just dinner.*

Torn between the pull of her flesh and the conviction of her spirit, no notion of what the rest of this trip would bring, she knew she needed to be careful. So much more was at stake than she wanted to admit.

Chapter 33

"I have the right to do anything, you said, but not everything is beneficial.

-1 Corinthians 10:23

At exactly 8:00 p.m., a soft knock interrupted Danielle's thoughts. One last glance in the mirror and she was satisfied. The black dress she wore was an ode to understated sophistication. It hugged her figure in all the right places, the fabric flowing smoothly to create an effortlessly refined silhouette. The simplicity of the design spoke volumes about her quiet confidence, even as the butterflies in her stomach refused to settle.

This isn't just a business dinner, and you know it, a small voice whispered in the recesses of her thoughts.

When she opened the door, the sight of Dominic made her breath hitch. He stood there in a tailored navy suit that seemed almost sculpted to his form. The brilliant white shirt beneath complemented his warm complexion, and the undone tie at his collar gave him a vibe of relaxed sophistication.

Dominic's gaze swept over her, lingering just long enough to send a warmth spreading across her skin. "You look stunning."

Danielle forced herself to maintain composure, even as her cheeks warmed. "Thank you." "You clean up pretty well yourself."

His chuckle was quiet, intimate. He offered his arm, inviting her with a "Shall we?".

She slipped her hand into the crook of his arm. Every brush of their arms felt amplified, every shared glance a spark threatening to consume them.

The charged energy between them hummed in the confined space of the elevator. They arrived at their destination, a cosy, candlelit bistro tucked away from the bustling.

Dominic guided her to a table near the window, his hand briefly grazing hers as he pulled out her chair. The touch was fleeting but electric. Danielle concentrated on the menu, though the elegant script blurred slightly under her gaze.

A server approached to take their drink orders. Dominic ordered a glass of Bordeaux, then looked at her with a curious tilt of his head. "And for you?"

"A non-alcoholic, sparkling lemonade spritzer, please."

Dominic's brow lifted slightly. "You don't drink, do you? The few times we've had dinner, you've never ordered an alcoholic drink."

"No, I don't."

"Is that a biblical principle?"

"Not particularly," she replied, meeting his gaze. "The Bible doesn't prohibit drinking, but it speaks against drunkenness. To avoid temptation, I choose not to drink at all."

"Interesting. So, you're a woman of principles."

"I try to be," but as she spoke, a pang of unease settled in her chest. *You're not being guided by this principle now, are you?* Her smile lingered, but her thoughts were agitated as she wrestled with the contradiction between her words and her situation.

Their conversation moved to lighter topics as the evening unfolded. They shared stories of childhood mischief and favourite books, Danielle laughed more than she expected. Dominic, usually so guarded, revealed glimpses of the boy he once was.

The friction between them had softened into something warm, almost easy, and Danielle permitted herself to enjoy it, to pretend this was just a pleasant dinner between two colleagues. But as the clock neared 10:00 p.m., reality crept back in.

Dominic escorted her to her room, his presence a steadying force beside her. When they reached her door, the charged atmosphere from earlier returned, surrounding them. Dominic faced her, his eyes darker, more intense under the soft hallway light.

"Thank you for a beautiful evening."

"Thank you." Before she could step inside, Dominic leaned in, brushing a tender kiss against her cheek, dangerously close to her lips, and pulled her into a hug. Danielle stiffened, every instinct warning her to step back. But then, disregarding her misgivings, she melted into the hug, the warmth and security of his arms enveloping her.

This feels so right, she thought, but as the thought took root, another voice rose in protest. *And that's exactly why it's wrong.* Biblically, spiritually, she knew it was wrong, but her soul and her body were speaking an entirely distinct language, one that made it harder and harder to listen to the voice of the Holy Spirit.

Dominic pulled back slightly, his forehead resting against hers, the warmth between them lingering. "Goodnight, Danielle. Sleep well." The words were gentle, but even as he said them, he recognised the irony—because he knew sleep would evade him tonight.

Her breath hitched, and for a moment, she simply stared at him, as if trying to steady herself. "Goodnight," she finally managed, her voice barely above a whisper.

As soon as the door clicked shut behind her, Danielle sagged against it, pressing a hand to her chest as if that could steady the wild rhythm of her heart. Her thoughts spun in dizzying circles, unravelling faster than she could grasp them. The boundaries she had so carefully built—walls of logic, restraint, and self-preservation—were crumbling, and she knew it. Worse still, a part of her wasn't sure she wanted to stop it.

Danielle, what are you doing? She scolded herself. You're leading yourself down a slippery slope. What's it going to be next? She moved through her nightly routine mechanically, reciting her prayers but struggling to focus. "God, help me, please keep me from falling into something I'll regret."

But while she prayed, her thoughts betrayed her. They kept returning to Dominic. To his touch, his voice, the way he made her feel both seen and completely unravelled. And as she crawled into bed, torn between desire and conviction, she realised just how precarious her position had become.

Chapter 34

It is not that we are [so] competent as to consider anything [we do] as coming from ourselves, but our competence comes from God.

-2 Corinthians 3:5

The following morning, Danielle was positioned in front of the mirror, adjusting her blazer. Her fitted black suit gave her an air of professionalism. Today was about business, she reassured herself firmly, tucking away the events of the previous evening.

When she met Dominic in the lobby, his casual ease as he leaned against the marble pillar struck a contrast to her heightened focus. In his sleek grey suit, he looked every bit the cut-throat executive, but the warmth of his smile as she approached softened his otherwise sharp demeanour.

"You look ready to conquer the world," Dominic remarked, gesturing for her to join him at a table nearby.

"That's the plan," Danielle replied with a slight smile, pouring herself a cup of strong black coffee from their table.

They spent the next half hour reviewing the business proposal. Dominic had to admire her thoroughness. Her insights into the French market and her anticipation of potential challenges were razor sharp.

"You've really covered every angle."

"I like to be prepared." The quiet confidence had him smiling.

Shared focus marked the car ride to their destination. When they entered the grand lobby of the French corporation, a nervous flutter ran through Danielle, but the expertise of dealing with her nerves, which she'd honed over the years, quickly took over.

The meeting began with introductions, followed by a discussion of the contract, but it was Danielle's fluent French that immediately improved the mood. Her pronunciation and clear articulation caught the executives' attention, warming the room with a newfound ease.

Throughout the negotiation, Dominic led, but it was Danielle's keen observations that truly elevated their position. When a French executive raised a point about a critical clause, Danielle seamlessly stepped in, countering with well-reasoned suggestions, that balanced assertiveness and diplomacy.

She spotted a potential loophole, highlighted it tactfully, proposing revisions that not only closed the gap but also added mutual benefit. Her skilful handling of delicate points impressed the French team, and by the meeting's conclusion, they sealed the deal on more favourable terms.

As they exited the meeting, Dominic addressed her with unmistakable admiration. "You were incredible in there," he said. "We wouldn't have got those terms without you."

Danielle smiled warmly, a quiet pride shining through. "It's all by God's grace," she said simply. "Excellence in everything I do is how I reflect Him."

The French CEO caught up with them, extending a dinner invitation to celebrate the deal. Danielle deferred to Dominic, exchanging a glance with him.

"Of course," Dominic smoothly responded, "we'd be delighted."

He glanced at her. "Dinner should be interesting."

Chapter 35

Control [Discipline] yourselves and be ·careful [alert]! The devil, your enemy,
·goes around [prowls] like a roaring lion looking for someone to ·eat [devour].

-1 Peter 5:8

Heads turned briefly as the pair entered the restaurant, their aura naturally demanding attention. Danielle's burgundy dress skimmed her figure, the deep colour accentuating her natural beauty. Her loose locs framed her face, and a simple gold necklace rested against her collarbone, adding a sense of effortless chic.

Dominic, in a sharp black suit, placed a light hand on the small of her back, guiding her toward the table where Monsieur Laroque and the other executives awaited them.

The evening progressed smoothly, punctuated by laughter and light conversation, until Monsieur Laroque's playful question disrupted the rhythm.

"So, Dominic, Danielle," he remarked, "this chemistry between you two, is it purely professional?"

Danielle froze. Before she could muster a response, Dominic replied smoothly, "It's strictly business."

Monsieur Laroque chuckled, clearly unconvinced. "Ah, but you would make a stunning couple," he added with a wink.

Dominic's fingers slipped into hers, under the table, his grip warm and steady. The gesture startled her, the unspoken intimacy of it sending a rush of emotion through her.

It was deliberate, possessive, and undeniably personal. She grappled with the significance of the moment, torn between the thrill of his touch and the heavy implications it carried.

Before she could dwell on it further, Dominic's phone buzzed, pulling him away. When he rose from the table, Laroque leaned closer, his tone shifting from playful to serious.

"Danielle, we're very impressed with you," he declared earnestly. "Your professionalism, your skills and knowledge of the French market is remarkable. It's rare to meet someone as capable."

"I appreciate it," she responded softly, unsure of where the conversation was heading.

Laroque lowered his voice. "We have an opening in our French division, overseeing international accounts. I believe you would be perfect for the role. I'd like you to consider it." He handed her his card, his expression earnest. "Take your time and think it over."

Danielle blinked, astonished. "I hadn't considered leaving Pascale & Pascale."

"I understand, but opportunities like this don't come often," Laroque rebutted.

Before she could respond, Dominic returned. She slipped the card into her purse discreetly, the significance of the offer settling in her mind. As the meal ended, they all shook hands and parted ways with the French executives, who once again praised Danielle for her performance. Laroque gave her one last meaningful look before they left, a silent reminder of the opportunity he had placed before her.

The ride to the hotel was steeped in a silence that was anything but peaceful. Lost in thought, Dominic replayed Vivienne's earlier words in his head. The timing of her call was no coincidence. Barbara had clearly fed her the information, knowing that he was in Paris with Danielle. *I miss you;* she had said. But it was more than just nostalgia; it was a deliberate move, a reminder of the past that she knew would unsettle him. Her call automatically brought Isabella to the forefront.

And then there was Monsieur Laroque's comment during dinner. *"You would make a stunning couple."* He said it casually, but it landed like a stone in Dominic's chest. *Did they look like a couple?* He had denied it, of course, but the chemistry between them was undeniable, even without the labels or formalities. There was something in the way their eyes searched for each other, the way their bodies seemed attuned to each other even in silence.

And then there was that moment, his possessive action of intertwining their hands beneath the table. *What had that been about?* It carried an unspoken message, a claim. For someone like him, always so controlled, it was a slip, one that revealed more than words ever could. The question was, what did it mean for them now?

Meanwhile, Danielle pondered Laroque's offer and Dominic's strange behaviour, since the phone call. When they reached the hotel, Dominic paused outside Danielle's door. "I have something for you," he stated, breaking the silence. "A thank you gift for your tireless work. Come, it's in my suite."

Inside his suite, he handed her an elegantly wrapped box. Danielle opened it to reveal a delicate pearl necklace. Her breath caught. "Dominic, this is too much," she protested. "You didn't have to."

"You deserve it." He moved nearer. "May I?" he asked softly. Dominic's gaze softened as he signalled for her to turn after taking the necklace from the box. Danielle complied, her breath hitching as she experienced the warmth of his presence behind her.

The cool touch of the pearls sent a shiver through her as he clasped the necklace with deliberate care, his fingers brushing lightly against her nape. The fleeting contact an unspoken promise, leaving her skin tingling.

"Look," he murmured, gesturing to the mirror. "It's beautiful. You're beautiful."

Danielle stared at their reflection, but the image before her faded into the background, eclipsed by the heat of his nearness, the warmth of his hand and the ghost of his breath tracing across her skin. Heat radiated from him, a silent invitation she could feel more than see.

His gaze remained fixed on her, intense and unwavering, testing, tempting, silently asking for permission, to close the distance, to cross the fragile line between restraint and passion.

What would it feel like if I just leaned into him? The thought slid into her mind unbidden, and for a fleeting moment, she imagined what it would be like to give in to the attraction that had been simmering between them. But then, a voice warned her: *Danielle, you're playing with fire, again!* "Thank you, Dominic, it's beautiful."

Dominic examined her intently, his expression carefully unreadable. Her wide, trusting eyes betrayed her innocence, a truth he recognised instantly. He'd been with enough women to distinguish between the practiced allure of experience and the raw, unguarded emotions she couldn't hide.

He knew, without doubt, that if he desired, he could shatter every one of her carefully constructed barriers, dispel her hesitations, and make her his tonight. The thought sent a wave of heat through him, but his respect for her swiftly tempered it.

Danielle's faith and unwavering principles were not just aspects of her personality, they were the foundation of who she was. They shaped her decisions, and that set her apart from anyone he'd ever known.

Dominic understood that crossing her boundaries would not only violate her trust but also compromise the very values that rendered her so remarkable to him. It wasn't solely restraint; it was about honouring the woman she was, her individuality and her steadfast faith.

For now, he would hold himself back, even if it meant resisting the pull that threatened to consume them both. Because Danielle deserved nothing less than respect, and he wasn't willing to tarnish what they had by succumbing to a few minutes of selfish desire.

"So, do you think we'd make a great couple?"

The question hung unanswered, heavy and loaded with meaning. He stared intently, awaiting her answer, and Danielle could feel the pull between them: dangerous, intoxicating and undeniably real. Her heartbeat quickened and as she searched for words, a scripture flashed in her mind: *"Watch and pray that you may not enter into temptation."* (Matthew 26:41).

"I think, that's a question for another day," as she stepped away from him.

He paused for the shortest of moments before stepping back. "I'll walk you to your room."

At her door, he paused. "Goodnight, Danielle."

"Goodnight, Dominic," she whispered.

The pearls around her neck suddenly felt heavy, almost suffocating. You're playing with fire. The warning echoed in her mind, relentless and unshakable. With a shaky breath, she sank into a chair, her fingers knotting together in a silent plea for strength. To resist, to hold her ground and to keep herself from stepping too close to the flames that threatened to consume her.

Chapter 36

We must hold on to the hope we have, never hesitating to tell people about it. We can trust God to do what he promised.

-Hebrews 10:23

The subsequent day, the pair walked side by side, the Eiffel Tower stretching against the blue sky, the Seine River glistening under the afternoon sun, and cobbled streets whispering centuries-old stories beneath their feet.

Dominic had arranged an extra day in Paris, a gesture that felt both thoughtful and dangerous to Danielle. The undercurrent between them both thrilled and unnerved her.

At the Louvre, they admired masterpieces in shared silence, their footsteps echoing softly in the grand halls. In the Luxembourg Gardens, the vibrant blooms appeared to reflect the emotions bubbling beneath the surface—beautiful, complex, and fragile.

Dominic's attentiveness caught her off guard. He pointed out architectural details, shared anecdotes from his past visits and drawing uninhibited laughter from her. But Danielle remained cautious, guarding her heart against the day's almost surreal perfection.

As twilight descended, washing the city in a warm amber glow, they entered an intimate restaurant. Over dinner, they discussed travel, work, the conversation flowing effortlessly. But as night fell, and the candlelight flickered between them, Danielle noticed Dominic's preoccupation.

Finally, after dessert, he made a decision. "I had a great day with you," he whispered. "I've needed this downtime for a long time. Would it be possible for us to spend more time together?"

Danielle felt a flutter in her chest, but she kept her gaze steady. "What do you mean?"

"I'm captivated by you, Danielle," Dominic admitted, his voice low and vulnerable. "But every time I think I'm ready to move on, Isabella..." His voice faltered, his hands clutched the table's edge as though to anchor himself.

His confession laid between them like a cloud, dense with unspoken emotions and the gravity of what it meant. Danielle's instinct was to comfort him, but she hesitated, unsure of how to proceed without crossing his boundaries.

Finally, she reached out, her fingers brushing his hand before resting atop it. "Do you wish to talk about it?" she asked gently.

Dominic lifted his gaze, his dark eyes stormy with grief and guilt. "She died in a car accident," his voice barely audible. "It was after a charity event. I stayed behind to handle some last-minute business and she drove home alone."

Danielle's chest tightened as he recounted the event of the night, his voice slow and deliberate, as though each word spoken was easing the weight he could no longer carry. He described the wet roads, the slick curve, and the tree that took Isabella's life. His voice cracked, and he paused as he fought to maintain control. "I should have been with her. I should have driven her home."

Danielle's eyes stung with unshed tears as she listened. His self-reproach was profound. She tightened her hold on his hand, willing him to feel the comfort she offered. "It wasn't your fault," she whispered, her voice quivering. "You couldn't have known."

"It doesn't matter," Dominic said sharply. "She's gone because I wasn't there and that's something I'll carry with me forever."

Danielle stood and moved to his side, her heart aching as she wrapped her arms around him. Initially, he resisted; however, he relaxed, resting his head on her shoulder. His grief poured out in silent waves, and she held him, her own tears slipping down her cheeks as she shared in his pain.

"You're not to blame, Dominic." "The pain and regret you're holding on to can heal if you give it to God."

Upon hearing God's name, Dominic tensed, and pulled back slightly. His eyes, still red, flickered with something unreadable. "Why are you so convicted about God?" he asked, his voice rough but curious.

"Because I know who He is," Danielle replied softly. "I know the sacrifice He made for me through his son Jesus Christ and I know He's the only one who can heal the wounds you're carrying."

Dominic's expression shifted, conflict and curiosity shadowing his features.

"I know you have doubts," Danielle continued gently, "but if we're going to have a future together, like you've alluded to, you must consider it."

Dominic nodded slowly, his gaze dropping to the floor. "Thank you for listening. We should return to the hotel. Our taxi leaves at 7:00 a.m. tomorrow. I'll meet you in the lobby at 6:30 for coffee and a light breakfast," his voice thick with emotion.

Back at the hotel, Danielle stood by her door, watching Dominic retreat to his own room. Her heart ached for him, for the brokenness he carried and the walls he'd built. But she realised she couldn't save him. Only God could and she had felt his immediate withdrawal when she mentioned God.

So, what's your plan, Danielle? How long will you wait for his decision regarding Christ? How many more times will you flirt with temptation before giving in? She couldn't dismiss the quiet conviction stirring within her. She had prayed for clarity, for God's guidance, and now she felt the answer beginning to take shape.

In the hotel lobby, the following morning, Dominic waited, his bearing imposing even in the early morning light. His usual confidence muted, replaced by a quiet intensity as he offered Danielle a subdued smile as she joined him.

"Good morning."

Danielle returned the greeting with a nod, her own smile restrained and they walked together to grab a quick bite and coffee, their exchanges polite but careful.

The atmosphere between them felt different now, a delicate balance of unspoken emotions and professional purpose. The cab ride to the airport went by in a reflective silence and the early morning streets of Paris, once alive with romance and possibility, now seemed distant.

Danielle stared out the window, her thoughts racing. Dominic occasionally looked her way, his gaze heavy with questions he was hesitant to ask.

Once they boarded the plane, Dominic broke the quiet first. "Last night," he began, his voice measured, "I've never really talked about Isabella like that before."

Danielle looked at him, her expression compassionate. "I could tell," she whispered. "But I'm glad you did. Sometimes, sharing our pain is the first step to healing."

Dominic nodded, though he kept his eyes trained on the seat ahead of him. "I feel different, letting it out. But it's strange. I feel like everything's going to changed now."

Danielle hesitated before she asked, "Would you like things to be different?"

Dominic's dark eyes met hers. "I don't know," he admitted. "I meant it when I said I'm captivated by you. You're unlike anyone I've ever met, however, I don't know what that means for me or for us."

"Dominic, there is something between us, but you're still carrying wounds that need time to heal, and I have convictions that I can't compromise. It's not just about attraction, it's about alignment of our lives and our beliefs, and right now, we're in different places."

"What if I'm not sure?"

Danielle held his gaze, searching for the meaning behind his words. "Unsure about us or God?"

He hesitated, then answered quietly, "Both."

"It's okay to be unsure about us, Dominic. You're human. But about God, your salvation, that's different. With God, there's no middle ground. You're with Him or against Him."

He nodded slowly, processing her words. "I understand. I'll consider it."

The conversation drifted to work, the success of their deal and upcoming plans for the week, but the earlier exchange remained a discordant note in their unfinished melody.

As the plane descended into London, the first rays of dawn painted the skyline in soft orange hues. Dominic surveyed the city, then turned to Danielle. "Back to reality," he muttered regretfully.

Danielle nodded, her spirit burdened with the uncertainty of what lay ahead. "Back to reality," she echoed quietly.

Chapter 37

God, you give true peace to people who depend on you, to those who trust in you.

-Isaiah 26:3

The soft hum of worship filled the church as the congregation sang together in harmony. Danielle sat near the middle, surrounded by familiar faces, yet a deep unease pressed on her chest. It was a disconnection she couldn't shake, a chasm that had grown since her return from Paris.

Her trip with Dominic had left her spirit heavy, burdened with thoughts she hadn't dared to fully confront. She had crossed no obvious lines, there had been no physical sin, but her thoughts and emotions told a different story. She had let herself drift toward desires that were incompatible with the life God had called her to live.

Lust. The word cut through her consciousness, and a knot formed in Danielle's stomach. She had rationalised her actions in Paris, telling herself it was harmless, that her feelings weren't wrong. But now, sitting in the presence of God, a deep conviction settled over her.

It wasn't what she had not done; it was about the thoughts she had entertained, the emotions she allowed to take precedence. Sin was more than action. It included our hidden thoughts, the truth buried in our hearts, that no one but God saw.

She bowed her head, seeking solace, but found discomfort. Memories replayed unbidden, the glances, the touches, the flutter of her heart whenever Dominic was near. She felt exposed, her own conscience shining a light on her actions. Her eyes filled with tears as she whispered, "Lord, I'm sorry. I let my emotions take over, and I drifted from You. Please, forgive me. I want nothing to come between us."

The worship faded into silence as the pastor approached the pulpit. Danielle wiped her eyes, murmuring a prayer. "God, please... reveal my path to me."

Pastor Ike began his sermon, his warm yet authoritative voice commanding attention.

"Today's topic is building strong homes and families." He paused, letting the weight of his words settle before he continued.

"The state of the family dictates the state of our society. There is a direct correlation between an unruly society and the prevalence of broken homes. And those broken homes, more often than not, stem from the decisions people make when choosing a husband or wife."

His voice carried conviction, each word landing with deliberate impact, as he urged the congregation to reflect on the foundation of relationships and their lasting consequences. Danielle sat up. She hadn't expected the message to feel so personal.

"Marriage is one of the most significant choices a person can make, yet it's often approached with far less care than it deserves," Pastor Ike continued, his voice steady with conviction.

"People rush in, driven by fleeting emotions, superficial attractions, or societal pressures, without truly considering the long-term consequences. But a solid marriage isn't just about love—it's about shared values, mutual respect, and a foundation built on God's principles."

He let the words settle, his gaze sweeping across the congregation. "Love alone is not enough. It must be anchored in something deeper, something lasting." Quiet reigned in the church, every eye fixed on him as he continued. "When we choose a partner based on worldly standards, wealth, appearance, status, we set ourselves up for instability. A house built on sand cannot withstand the storms of life."

"But when you build on a rock on the veracity of God's Word, on prayer and on seeking His guidance, your family becomes a stronghold, a source of light in a dark world. Feelings, physical attraction, and those initial butterflies lead many women, even Christian women, to marry the wrong person."

Danielle shifted on the pew, her heart skipping a beat at her pastor's words. The butterflies she'd felt around Dominic came rushing back, along with the confusion they brought.

"But permit me to tell you something about those butterflies. They're called butterflies for a reason. Because, just like butterflies, they have a short lifespan! One minute, they're fluttering around all pretty and the next splat right on the windshield of reality!"

The congregation chuckled as he carried on, "That thrill, that excitement, that chemistry? It's like a sugar rush fun while it lasts, but eventually, you're just left with... a crash. So, when the butterflies take off, what are you left with? Hopefully, something other than just a bunch of empty candy wrappers!"

Laughter rippled across the room, lightening the serious tone of his message.

"Now, let me tell you, church, those qualities that sweep you off your feet in the beginning? They can just as easily sweep you under the rug in marriage. The same man who showers you with gifts during courtship might frustrate you later when he's spending money on everything except the bills. Did you like those surprise concert tickets when you were dating? Well, not so fun when the electric bill is the surprise."

Laughter erupted as he continued, "You have to be wise, ladies and gentlemen. The quality of your marriage depends on the quality of the person you choose to marry. And remember, you can't return a spouse like a faulty toaster!"

Danielle felt a knot forming in her stomach. Her thoughts wandered back to Dominic, his charm, his intensity, the undeniable attraction between them. But was that enough?

"God designed marriage to bring out His glory. It's not just about love; it's about purpose. There are questions you need to ask before you make such a life-altering decision. Your marriage, after your salvation, is the most important decision you will make."

"Here are a few questions every wise woman should ask before committing to a man. The same is also for men, but today I'm focussing on the ladies!" Pastor continued.

"Question one." "Why me? What tangible qualities can he see in you? Is it just your beauty, or does he value your character, your spirit, your calling?"

Danielle scribbled the first question down, feeling a lump rise in her throat. Did Dominic see beyond her outward appearance, beyond the initial attraction? Did he value her character, her spirit, her calling?

"Question 2." "Do I know him well enough? Are you friends? Do you know his thoughts on God, the role of a woman, finances, children? Can you talk to him about your values?" Danielle swallowed hard. They had shared moments of vulnerability, but had they had not delved into their core values.

"Question 3." "His influences. Who are they? Who does he listen to? Who are his friends, his mentors? It's a law of life that you become who you follow. Does he have someone who holds him accountable? A man without who does not have a head, is dangerous."

Danielle's heart pounded harder. The question struck a deep chord. Who guided Dominic? Did anyone hold him accountable? He was powerful, independent, but did he have anyone he answered to? Without God as his head, could he truly lead a family? She already knew the answer, but facing it felt like tearing open a wound she hadn't the courage to treat.

"Question 4." "Is he compatible with me? Do you share the same values, the same beliefs? Because, church, I must say, physical attraction is only one piece of the puzzle. Compatibility in your spirit, your purpose, your beliefs that's what will hold a marriage together."

As the questions poured out, Danielle sensed the Holy Spirit pressing into her heart. Every word felt meant for her, urging her to examine not just Dominic, but herself, her faith, and her future. She bit her lip, fighting the emotion rising within her.

"Young women, if you aspire to build strong homes, you must be wise in your decision. Avoid being led by fleeting infatuations. Let the Spirit of God, wisdom, and discernment guide you."

"So today, I challenge you: look at your home, your choices, your priorities. Are they aligned with God's vision for your family or the one you plan to have? When we get the family right, we lay the foundation for a stronger, more righteous society."

When the service ended, Danielle lingered in her seat, clutching her notebook. The questions played over and over in her mind, each one carving out a deeper conviction. And now, she needed to confront the truth, no matter how painful it might be. "God, please enlighten me." Deep down, she knew God had given her the clarity she prayed for. All that remained was finding the courage to act on it.

Chapter 38

"Even now," said the Lord, "Turn and come to Me with all your heart [in genuine repentance], With fasting and weeping and mourning [until every barrier is removed and the broken fellowship is restored]"

-Joel 2:12

Danielle began the new week with a heavy heart. Her pastor's words echoed in her mind, offering the clarity she had sought but also feared.

The butterflies she once felt around Dominic now seemed weak, their fleeting nature a stark reminder that they weren't a foundation for anything real or lasting.

As she stepped into the Pascale & Pascale building, the usual buzz of energy felt oppressive rather than invigorating. She could only imagine how Barbara had spent the past few days sowing seeds of discord in her absence.

Each strained smile, each thinly veiled greeting, carried an undercurrent of judgment. Danielle felt like she was navigating a minefield, one misstep away from detonation. When she arrived at her desk, her chest was tight with anxiety.

She inhaled deeply, trying to shake the unease, but her mind kept circling back to the afternoon meeting. She wasn't sure what was more daunting, the professional challenges or the personal speculation swirling around her and Dominic.

At precisely 2:00 p.m., Danielle entered the boardroom, bracing herself. The subdued chatter in the room came to an abrupt halt as she stepped in. Dominic was already there, composed as always, his presence commanding attention as he stood at the head of the table.

"Thank you all for your hard work while Ms Thompson and I were in Paris," Dominic began, his tone businesslike but warm. "The trip was a success, and I'm pleased to report that we secured the deal on terms better than expected."

Polite applause followed, but Danielle couldn't ignore the suspicious glances exchanged between some of her colleagues.

When her gaze met Barbara's, a chill ran through her. The woman's smirk was calculated, dripping with quiet satisfaction, her fingers drumming lightly on the table—a silent display of victory.

Meanwhile, Dominic continued, unaware of the undercurrent of tension.

"I'd also like to congratulate Danielle on her exceptional contributions during the trip. She helped to secure this deal, and her proposal for an apprenticeship program for female ethnic minorities has received approval."

Danielle barely had time to process the significance of his words before she felt the weight of the room shift—a mix of genuine acknowledgment, unspoken resentment, and Barbara's thinly veiled hostility pressing in from all sides. Danielle had worked tirelessly on that project, and its approval meant the world to her. But the victory was short-lived.

"Congratulations, Danielle," Barbara said, her tone dripping with false sincerity. "Looks like you've been quite busy... both in and out of the office."

A ripple of low laughter passed through the room—subtle, but unmistakable. The insinuation hung in the air, heavy and deliberate.

Danielle's face burned, though she forced herself to remain composed. The weight of their judgment pressed in, unspoken but suffocating.

Meanwhile, Dominic, oblivious to the undercurrent, simply smiled warmly at her.

"Great work, Ms Thompson."

His praise should have felt like validation, but it only made the whispers sting more.

"Thank you, Mr Pascale." The meeting concluded, and as the room emptied, Dominic called out, "Ms Thompson, a moment, please."

Her stomach knotted as she stayed behind. She could feel Barbara's condemnation as she left, no doubt feeding the rumour mill.

Following the closing of the door, Dominic's demeanour softened. "I simply wanted to thank you again. The work you did in Paris was exceptional."

Danielle forced a smile. "I was only doing my job."

Dominic studied her, concern flickering in his gaze. "You seemed distracted during the meeting. Is something wrong?"

Danielle hesitated, the temptation to unload her frustrations warring with her instinct to handle things alone.

After a brief pause, she forced a small smile. "It's nothing," she said finally. "Just the usual stress."

She hoped the answer was enough to satisfy his curiosity, but the way Dominic's eyes lingered on her, searching, told her he wasn't convinced.

Dominic didn't press further. Instead, he slid his hand around the back of her neck, his fingers curling gently as he drew her closer. His touch was firm yet careful, anchoring her as he leaned in and placed a soft, lingering kiss at the corner of her lips.

The gesture was intimate, deliberate, charged with unspoken emotion. It wasn't just a touch, it was an invitation, silent yet undeniable, urging her to meet him halfway. She only needed to tilt her head slightly to make the boundaries between them disappear completely.

Danielle's breath caught as her mind screamed at her to pull away. This is wrong. You know this is wrong, her mind warring with her heart as the moment hung precariously between them. In the end, it was Dominic who stepped back, disappointment clear in his eyes.

Without a word, Danielle turned and walked away, her steps steady but her spirit in turmoil. The weight of her emotions and convictions pressed on her as she reached the solitude of her home.

That night, Danielle fell to her knees in prayer. Tears streamed down her face. "Father, forgive me. I've let my emotions and desires lead me, and I've drifted from You. I've tried to justify this situation, but I see now that I've been walking a dangerous path."

Danielle resolved she would fast for the next three days, to crucify the desires that had been plaguing her heart, the subtle temptation to justify Dominic's disbelief in God, her wavering feelings for him and her failure to trust in God's plan. She had to break the spiritual stronghold of the spirit of lust threatening to overwhelm her. *"So I say, walk by the Spirit and you will not gratify the desires of the flesh." - Galatians 5:16.*

She needed to realign her thoughts with God's truth to strengthen her mental resolve and free her mind from clutter, allowing her to confront and bring all her emotional turmoil before God for healing. She dedicated her mornings to prayer and meditating on scriptures like Matthew 26:41: *"Watch and pray so that you will not fall into temptation. The spirit is willing, but the flesh is weak."*

By the third day, a renewed sense of peace washed over Danielle. Though the struggle wasn't over, she found her anchor in God's truth. As she ended her fast, she whispered, "Lord, guide my steps. Help me honour you in all I do."

Chapter 39

But Samuel replied: "Does the Lord delight in burnt offerings and sacrifices as much as in obeying the Lord? To obey is better than sacrifice and to heed is better than the fat of rams."

-Samuel 15:22

By Thursday, the heaviness that had burdened Danielle earlier in the week was lifting. The Holy Spirit had been steadfast, bringing her repeatedly to 2 Corinthians 6:14: *"Do not be unequally yoked with unbelievers. For what partnership has righteousness with lawlessness? Or what fellowship has light with darkness?"* She felt more grounded, more in harmony with God's plan for her life.

That afternoon, she received an email from Monsieur Laroque.

Subject: Exciting Career Opportunity

Dear Danielle,

I hope this email finds you well.

Following our recent collaboration in Paris, I wanted to express how impressed we were with your exceptional work personally. Your expertise, professionalism and creativity throughout the meeting and your contributions did not go unnoticed.

With that in mind, I am pleased to extend to you a formal offer for a prestigious position within our organisation. We designed this role specifically to use your unique skills and experience so that you can significantly impact our team and our work. We are confident that this opportunity will not only align with your career aspirations, but also provide an exciting platform for your continued growth and success.

Attached, you will find the full details of the offer, including the job description, responsibilities and benefits package. Please take your time to review it thoroughly and reach out with questions or clarifications you may need.

We truly believe that you would be an invaluable asset to our team and are looking forward to the possibility of welcoming you aboard.

Warm regards,
Monsieur Laroque
CEO | Banque De Diamants

As she read the offer, Danielle felt an overwhelming sense of clarity. This was God's way of showing her the path she needed to take. The job offer wasn't just a career opportunity; it was a new beginning, a chance to leave behind the confusion and the tangled emotions she'd been wrestling with. The answer to her prayers was right in front of her.

She closed her eyes, whispering a prayer of thanks. "Thank You, Lord, for giving me this clarity. I know now what I need to do, and I trust you to guide me in this next step."

As she prepared for her meeting with Dominic, her heart ached with the action she was about to take. She prayed softly as she walked to his office, her voice barely audible: "Lord, give me the strength to do this Your way, not mine."

She knocked on the door, her breath steady despite the trembling in her chest. Dominic's deep voice called her in, and as she stepped inside, their eyes locked.

For a moment, Dominic was speechless. Danielle looked effortlessly poised in her simple but elegant dress. The air between them was thick with unspoken words, and Dominic, for the first time in weeks, knew with absolute certainty what he wanted: *Her.*

Before Danielle could speak, Dominic was across the room, his hands capturing hers, his touch warm and insistent. "Danielle," he began, his voice soft, almost pleaded. "Before you say anything, I need to say this. I'm ready. I'll even give your God a chance, if that's what it takes."

Danielle's heart twisted painfully. She felt the gravity of what he was offering, but more importantly, she recognised what this was: one ultimate test, a ploy by the enemy to throw her off course. She could feel the spiritual warfare at play. Just when she had received confirmation from God, the devil was throwing a curve ball. A few days earlier, she might have hesitated, might have allowed her emotions to guide her. But now, with God's clarity, she knew the truth.

"Dominic..." she began, her voice steady but tender, as she gently pulled her hands free. Her touch lingered, her thumb brushing his cheek in a soothing gesture. "Thank you for choosing me... for being willing to sacrifice so much. But..." She paused, her voice soft yet unwavering. "I'm sorry. We cannot be together."

Dominic blinked, his brow furrowing in confusion. "What?" he breathed out, his voice shaking. "Danielle, I'm willing to try. I'm ready to change."

"I know," she said, her voice calm but filled with compassion. "And I care about you, deeply. But our values, our beliefs, they're too far apart. I can't deny my physical and intellectual attraction to you, but we are unequally yoked."

Dominic's expression darkened, hurt flashing in his eyes. His voice hardened, a coldness creeping into his tone. "Unequally yoked? What the hell does that mean?" he spat, stepping back. "So, this is what your God is about? Making my life miserable?"

"Dominic," Danielle's voice softened even more, her heart aching at the hurt visible in his expression. She could feel the hurt radiating off him, the anger, the rejection. "Let me explain."

She took a deep breath, drawing strength from the scripture that had guided her all week. "In ancient times, farmers yoked oxen together with a wooden beam, a two-pronged fork to plough fields. Both oxen had to be equally strong and aligned, pulling in the same direction. If one ox was weaker or pulled in a different direction, the field wouldn't be ploughed properly. That would create chaos."

She met his gaze, her voice softening. "Dominic, we are in two different places. We'd be pulling in two different directions. It would only hurt us both. Over time, it would lead to frustration, resentment, and heartache."

Dominic stood frozen, staring at her. The silence was deafening.

"So that's it?" he asked, his voice clipped. "We can't be together? Because your God says so?"

Danielle reached into her purse, fighting back the tears welling in her eyes, and pulled out the resignation letter and the jewellery box containing the pearl necklace. She placed them gently on his desk.

"I cannot accept this gift," she whispered, her voice trembling but resolute. "And this is my resignation. I received a job offer from Monsieur Laroque's company, and I accepted."

The words hit Dominic like a physical blow. He jolted back, staring at her in disbelief. Slowly, he turned away, walking to the glass window overlooking the city. His hand rested against the cool pane, his reflection distorted in the fading evening light.

"You're leaving?" he asked hollowly. "Just like that? What about your apprenticeship initiative?"

Danielle swallowed hard, her heart breaking at his tone. "The initiative is dear to me. Move forward with it. It's an important project."

The silence stretched between them, suffocating. She could see the tension in his shoulders, the way his breathing had quickened. Finally, he spoke, his voice distant. "Thank you for your honesty," he said flatly. "I hope you find what you're looking for."

Danielle hesitated, her hand on the door. "Despite what you think, God loves you, Dominic," she said, her voice filled with quiet conviction. "I hope you'll give Him a chance to find you."

As she closed the door behind her, she heard it, the roar of anguish as Dominic swept everything off his desk. The sound of glass shattering echoed through the halls, and Danielle's tears finally spilled over as she hurried down the corridor. Her heart was heavy, but she knew she had made the right decision.

Dominic stood amidst the wreckage of his office, the shattered glass and scattered papers mirroring the chaos in his mind. His chest heaved as he tried to steady his breathing. She was gone. Just like Isabella.

The thought hit him with the force of a freight train, dredging up memories he had tried so hard to bury. Isabella's departure had been permanent, irrevocable. One moment, she was there vibrant, laughing, the light of his life and then she wasn't.

The accident had stolen her away without warning, leaving behind only a void that he had spent months trying to fill. It was grief in its purest, most devastating form, the kind that carved out pieces of your soul and left you hollow.

But this? Danielle's absence felt almost as crushing, as though the universe had conspired to wound him in the same way all over again. She wasn't gone in the physical sense, but the finality of her rejection, the resignation letter sitting starkly on his desk, made it clear she was out of his life. Unlike Isabella, whom fate took from him, Danielle chose to leave. That realisation cut deeper than he expected.

He sank into his chair, his head falling into his hands. The room felt cavernous, the air heavy with regret and frustration. With Isabella, he had grieved what could never be. With Danielle, circumstances forced him to confront what could have been.

She had offered him something more than attraction or fleeting passion; a glimpse of something he hadn't dared to hope for since Isabella a future, a partnership, a chance to heal.

And yet, he had lost her, too. His own choices, his reluctance to embrace the faith that defined her, had built an insurmountable wall between them. He had tried to meet her halfway, offering to "give her God a chance," but even as he said it, he had known it wasn't enough. She saw through him, saw the hollow promise for what it was, and refused to compromise the integrity of her beliefs.

It was maddening, the way she had walked away with such grace, such conviction. It left him feeling raw, exposed, and helpless. He wanted to blame her, to accuse her of being self-righteous or cold, but he couldn't.

Deep down, he respected her more for it. That was the irony of it all: her unwavering commitment to her faith, the very thing that separated them, was also what made her so extraordinary to him.

He glanced at the pearl necklace, still pristine in its box amidst the wreckage. It was a cruel reminder of what he had lost twice. The pearls, once intended as a token of affection, now seemed to symbolise the fragility of his connections. No matter how much he cared, no matter how much he tried, the women he loved always seemed to slip through his fingers.

Fate had taken Isabella. Conviction had taken Danielle. The loss felt identical: suffocating, inescapable, absolute.

Dominic leaned back in his chair, his gaze fixed on the ceiling as he let the silence envelop him. The ache in his chest didn't subside, but somewhere in the depths of his despair, a small voice stirred. It was the echo of Danielle's parting words: *"God loves you. I hope you'll give Him a chance to find you."*

He scoffed at the notion, yet the words lingered, refusing to fade. For the first time in years, he allowed himself to sit with the possibility. He wondered if something or someone larger existed. Is there anything that could fill the void Isabella left and soothe the pain reignited by Danielle's departure?

He didn't have the answers, but as he sat there in the wreckage of his office and his heart, a seed of curiosity bloomed. Maybe one day, he'd search for Danielle's God.

Chapter 40

"For I know the plans I have for you," declares the Lord, "plans to prosper you and not to harm you, plans to give you hope and a future."

-Jeremiah 29:11

Three years later

Danielle sat by the pool, her hands resting gently on her swollen belly, feeling the soft, rhythmic kicks of the life growing inside her. The warm sun bathed her skin and a gentle breeze stirred the surrounding air. Eyes closed, she savoured the peacefulness of the day and the quiet joy in her heart.

Across the pool, she saw her husband, François, smiling at her from where he stood, towel in hand, freshly out of the water. His tousled dark hair glistened in the sunlight, his powerful frame a constant reminder of how much God had blessed her. He was laughing with their close friends who had gathered for the afternoon, his laughter deep and warm, like him.

François wasn't just her husband; he was her partner in every sense. Together, they prayed over decisions, celebrated God's faithfulness, and supported each other's dreams. He regarded her as his equal in their shared faith, a fellow worker for Christ. She had never experienced such peace, such certainty of her destined place.

François caught her gaze. His smile softened and in that moment, the rest of the world faded away. It was just the two of them, wrapped in the love they had found through God's grace.

She said a silent prayer, "Thank you, Lord, for guiding me, for giving me the strength to follow your will. I am grateful for you blessing me with a man who is my equal in every way."

François walked over to her, kneeling beside her and resting his hand on her belly, feeling the solid movements beneath his fingers. His eyes, so full of love, searched hers and she knew without words how much he adored her and their unborn child.

"How are my two favourite people doing?" he asked, his voice soft and filled with affection.

"We're doing well," Danielle replied, her own voice just as tender. She placed her hand over his. "Just thinking about how blessed we are."

François kissed her gently, lingeringly on her lips, then whispered, "I'm the blessed one, Danielle."

She smiled, tears welling in her eyes, not from sadness but from the overwhelming joy of knowing she had followed the right path. Three years ago, standing in Dominic's office, facing one of the hardest decisions of her life, she couldn't have imagined the future God had prepared for her. She had trusted His plan, knowing that she had to follow His Word, even if it meant walking away from someone she had cared about deeply.

Dominic had been a significant chapter in her life—a chapter that taught her about faith, boundaries and trust in God's plan. She prayed that wherever he was; he had found his own path, perhaps even found his way to God.

God had been faithful, as He always was. He had brought François into her life when she least expected it—a man who shared her faith, her values and her love for Christ. Together, they built a life centred on God, filled with mutual respect, deep love, and joy. There were no compromises in their spiritual journey; equally yoked, walking in the same direction.

Under her hand, the gentle kicks snapped her back to the present, reminding her of the new life she had not only within her but also the life she had accepted when she yielded to God's plan. She looked out at the rippling water, its surface reflecting the sky, much like her life now mirrored God's promises.

As the baby kicked again, François chuckled. "I think we have a little athlete in there."

Danielle laughed softly. "Or a dancer."

"Either way," François said, "he or she is already so loved."

Danielle looked at him, her heart full. "Yes... and so am I."

She felt an overwhelming sense of contentment wash over her, a profound thankfulness that she had followed God's will, even when it was hard, even when she didn't know what lay ahead. His plans had always been more significant than her own and now she was living proof of His faithfulness.

As the sun dipped below the horizon, casting a golden glow over the water, Danielle whispered a last prayer, *"Thank you, Lord, for showing me that your ways are higher than mine. Your faithfulness has never failed me."*

François took her hand in his and they sat in comfortable silence, watching the sun disappear into the horizon. Whatever the future held, she knew they would face it together, with God at the centre of their lives.

The End

Dear Reader,

Thank you for taking the time to read *Unequally Yoked*. I trust its message has blessed and encouraged you. Within these pages, we've explored valuable lessons on marriage, family, work ethics and what it means to live a life set apart for God. I hope you have taken something meaningful away from this story.

If you are saved, I encourage you to continue living boldly for God, and to walk in His grace and purpose. If you unsaved or are uncertain about your faith, I urge you not to wait another day without Him in your life. To accept Jesus Christ as Lord and Saviour is the most important decision you will ever make; it is filled with peace, love, and eternal hope. If you feel led, I invite you to say the **Sinner's Prayer** below:

Dear God in heaven,

I come to You in the name of Jesus. I acknowledge that I am a sinner and I am sorry for my sins and the life I have lived. I ask for Your forgiveness. I believe that Your only begotten Son, Jesus Christ, shed His precious blood on the cross at Calvary and died for my sins. I am now willing to turn away from my sin. Your Word says that if we confess the Lord Jesus with our mouth and believe in our hearts that God raised Him from the dead, we shall be saved.

Lord Jesus, I open my heart to You. Come into my life and be my Lord and Saviour. Thank You for saving me and for giving me eternal life. In Jesus' name, I pray. Amen.

If you've prayed this prayer, welcome to the family of God! Your journey has just begun and I encourage you to connect with a Bible-believing church where you can grow in faith and community.

May God bless you abundantly

Ginna Andrew

Printed in Great Britain
by Amazon